Praise for Hazel Marshall

'Swashbuckling pirates, an unrequited love affair and mystery
magic make this a rollicking read'
Liverpool Echo

'*Troublesome Angels and Flying Machines* is a charming
and highly readable fancy'
TES

'An impressive debut from Hazel Marshall . . . this is
old-fashioned fare in the best tradition of adventure stories,
expertly paced and confidently written'
Sunday Herald

'An inventive hoot, fast moving and quite bonkers'
Families SE

'An entertaining and unusual story for younger
readers . . . the villains are excellent'
History Teaching Review

'An exciting debut novel . . . Intelligently written
and a real page-turner.'
Birmingham Post

Troublesome Angels
Race to the Rescue

Hazel Marshall

OXFORD
UNIVERSITY PRESS

OXFORD

UNIVERSITY PRESS

Great Clarendon Street, Oxford OX2 6DP

Oxford University Press is a department of the University of Oxford.
It furthers the University's objective of excellence in research, scholarship,
and education by publishing worldwide in

Oxford New York

Auckland Cape Town Dar es Salaam Hong Kong Karachi
Kuala Lumpur Madrid Melbourne Mexico City Nairobi
New Delhi Shanghai Taipei Toronto

With offices in

Argentina Austria Brazil Chile Czech Republic France Greece
Guatemala Hungary Italy Japan Poland Portugal Singapore
South Korea Switzerland Thailand Turkey Ukraine Vietnam

Oxford is a registered trade mark of Oxford University Press
in the UK and in certain other countries

British Library Cataloguing in Publication Data

Data available

ISBN-13: 978-0-19-272613-1
ISBN-10: 0-19-272613-7

1 3 5 7 9 10 8 6 4 2

Typeset by Newgen Imaging Systems (P) Ltd., Chennai, India
Printed by Cox & Wyman Ltd, Reading, Berkshire

For Mum and Dad, with love

Thanks to my agent Caroline Walsh and to my editors, Liz Cross and Polly Nolan, for being so supportive.

Many many thanks to all my friends and family for sharing the good and bad times.

And, finally, thanks to JB for taking me to the mountains and letting me find my own heartstone.

The people of the mountains say that once there was a girl and a boy who were in love. One day a fallen angel saw the girl and fell in love with her. But she loved the boy more than the angel. The angel killed the girl, took her heart, and buried it deep in the earth, covering it with a mountain and then with a coat of ice. If he could not have her heart then neither could her lover. They say her heart turned to stone and became . . . the heartstone.

It is said that the heartstone is deep blue with red undertones, but that it is covered in clear ice—like an eye filmed with tears.

And, as it was created with the emotions of passion, love, jealousy, and regret, the heartstone contains immense power. It is believed that anyone who holds it will have the ability to change one thing. But it can only be freed by a special person, the Adept.

> To win this stone the Adept must
> First of all, fly like a bird
> Speak with the angels
> And love like no other . . .

Chapter 1

'There she is! Straight ahead!'

The cry came from high up on the mast, from the crow's nest.

'Maintain course!' shouted Antonio, the pirate captain.

Blanco rushed to the side and looked to where the boy was pointing. On the horizon, barely visible, was another ship. It had to be the golden ship—the one they were chasing.

'Is it them?' he asked. 'Will we catch them?'

'If we're lucky,' replied Antonio, with a flash of his gold teeth.

Blanco glanced at the sky at Antonio's words. Over the past year he'd discovered that luck wasn't always what it seemed. Sometimes luck had to do with angels. Three angels in particular—Azaz and Micha who brought good luck and Rameel who brought bad.

'Is it the Count? Is it them?' asked Gump, joining Blanco.

Antonio was bellowing out orders. He wanted more sail. He wanted to move faster. He wanted to catch that ship and board it.

'I think so,' Blanco replied briefly. He still hadn't forgiven his great-uncle for putting them all in danger in the first place. If Gump hadn't written those letters twenty years ago then none of this would have happened. Blanco might never have fallen out with the Count, Eva would never have been captured on their return to Venice, and they wouldn't be trying to rescue her now.

With the extra sail the pirate ship gained fast on its prey. The golden ship would soon be close enough to board. Blanco could see Eva standing on deck, her blonde hair flying in the wind.

'Eva!' he shouted, waving his hands wildly above his head. There was no reaction. Probably she hadn't heard him. But surely she must be able to see him? Who could ignore a pirate ship bearing down on them? Why didn't she wave back?

'There's something wrong,' muttered Antonio. 'Something's not right.'

Why wasn't there more activity on the other ship? They were about to be attacked by pirates! At the very least, they should be preparing to defend themselves.

'It's a trap,' Antonio cried. Then louder. 'It's a trap! Turn about! Turn about!'

'Are you mad?' cried Blanco, grabbing Antonio's arm. 'We've been chasing them for days! You can't turn back now!'

Antonio pushed Blanco away roughly. 'Turn about!' he shouted again. He grabbed the wheel and frantically began spinning it anti-clockwise. His crew hauled on the sails, helping to turn the ship around. The ship creaked and groaned as it was turned against its will.

Blanco was furious as he staggered to his feet. Gump was hanging on to a rope trying to keep his balance as the pirate ship swerved violently from side to side. It couldn't be a trap. His friends the angels

x

would have warned him. They'd brought them this far, after all.

'Not one feather,' said Rameel's malicious voice. 'Don't move even one feather unless you want Micha to die.'

The angel Azaz could barely contain his fury. His wings trembled with the effort of controlling his anger but he knew he had to. He glared at Rameel but the dark angel just smiled at him and tightened his grasp on the golden angel in his arms.

Rameel held Micha's wings in a tight grip. Her golden face looked strained but it was more from anger than pain.

'Do you know,' Rameel asked Eva conversationally, 'how to kill an angel?'

Eva refused to react to Rameel's taunting. She continued staring at the pirate ship. She was sure she could see Blanco.

'It's quite difficult,' Rameel continued, 'but there are ways.'

'Let her go,' said Azaz. 'I won't warn Blanco about Count Maleficio's plans. Just let Micha go.'

Rameel ignored him and continued talking to Eva.

'Maybe I won't tell you,' he said. 'You might use it against me. But if Azaz moves you might just find out.'

Antonio was trying to keep his ship under control as it turned.

'What kind of trap?' Blanco shouted at him.

Antonio didn't need to reply because the very next moment the question was answered. A streak of fire flew over their heads followed by a thunderous roar. Everyone ducked. When Blanco looked up again it was to find the mainsail on fire.

'Wh-what was that?' asked Gump, torn between wonder and fear.

'That,' said Blanco in disbelief, 'was the beast. I thought we had destroyed it on Malta, but he must have built another one.'

That was the beast! Blanco had told him about a machine that the Count had invented which could send fire and thunder hurtling across the skies. He had seen something like it years before at the court of the Great Khan but never since. Of course the Count himself hadn't managed to make it work. Blanco had finished it for him before realizing just how destructive it would be.

'It's demons!' cried one of the pirates. He fell to his knees and looked up to the sky. 'Save us!'

Antonio kicked him. 'Get up!' he shouted. 'Or I'll give you something worse than demons to worry about. Put that fire out!'

Terrified, the young pirate jumped to his feet. Blanco ran to help, knowing it was imperative they put the fire out before it reached the deck. Thanks to Antonio's evasive actions the damage was nowhere near as bad as it could have been. Had they still been heading straight for the ship, the strike from the beast could have gone into the bow and they would have sunk.

They hauled down the sail, soaking it with water at the same time. It was hard and heavy work. But, despite their efforts, by the time the fire was under control the mainsail hung in tatters. They immediately began to raise the spare sail but they were losing time.

❧ 4 ❧

The golden ship was in full flight and the gap between the two was widening as they worked.

'I can't believe Azaz didn't warn us!' said Blanco.

The others said nothing. Blanco was the only one apart from Eva who could talk to the angels and the rest had a difficult time believing in them.

'The ship is still in sight,' said Antonio grimly. He was furious. Now that his ship had been attacked the chase had become personal. No one attacked his ship and got away with it. Especially not when it was done in such a cowardly way, not even daring to set foot on deck to fight for what they wanted. Secretly, Antonio knew that if he had had the beast then he would have done the same thing but he wasn't going to admit that out loud. 'As long as we keep them in sight we won't lose them.'

Gump frowned as a wisp or two of mist dawdled in front of his eyes, teasing him. He looked behind him and groaned.

The others turned and Blanco stared in disbelief. By the time he faced the front again, the sea fog had obliterated the horizon. Soon the golden ship—and Eva—had disappeared into its cloudy embrace.

As the mist came down, Count Maleficio and Luca Ferron nearly hugged each other with joy.

'Well done!' cried a jubilant Luca. 'They can't follow us now!'

Count Maleficio smiled in delight. 'If only they hadn't swung round then we would have hit them full on!'

'Still,' continued Luca, smiling beatifically, 'we've made things much more difficult for them.'

The Count hugged his silver cloak tightly round him and smiled with glee at the small round man in front of him. 'With luck they'll all sink,' he gloated. He had no love for Blanco or his great-uncle and nothing gave him more pleasure than the thought of them lying under the sea being nibbled on by fish. Blanco Polo had an unfortunate habit of scuppering all his plans. Having kidnapped Eva from Venice, the Count didn't want Blanco following them and preventing them from reaching the Blue Mountain, their final destination.

Count Maleficio and Luca Ferron believed that Eva was the adept and therefore the only one who could release the heartstone from its imprisonment deep within the mountains of Badakhshan. Nothing, and especially not Blanco, was going to prevent them from gaining the ultimate power that the heartstone would bring.

'And with this mist they'll have no way of knowing where we're heading.'

'Yes they will,' burst out Eva smugly. She had been listening to their conversation. 'They've always known where you were going. We heard you in Barcelona saying that the ship was bound for Acre. They'll catch us there if not before.'

Luca Ferron stopped smiling for a moment. His cheeks immediately sagged and his face took on an uneven look. When he wasn't smiling the top half of his face was too big for the bottom half.

'We should change the route,' he said. 'We can't risk them catching us up.'

'And with the mist,' added the Count, stroking his

chin with a long bony finger, 'they will assume we have continued straight on. Besides, the beast has broken and I may not be able to fix it until we reach land.'

Eva and Magdalena stared at each other in horror. If they changed direction now then Blanco might never find them again. Eva wished she had never opened her mouth.

'Head north!' shouted Luca to the captain.

The great ship changed direction.

'We have to keep heading for Acre,' said Blanco firmly. 'That's where the golden ship is heading.'

Gump nodded in agreement. Acre was the port town of the Holy Land. It was where he had started his journey to Badakhshan forty years before. Badakhshan was where the Blue Mountain was, and where the Count and Luca were going.

Antonio shook his head. 'I keep telling you that Acre is not as it was when your great-uncle was there forty years ago,' he explained. 'It was completely destroyed twenty years ago. It's an abandoned city. No one goes there now.'

'But that's where they said they were going!' said Blanco. 'In Barcelona.' Eva and Blanco had first escaped from the Count and Luca Ferron months ago in the port of Barcelona after Blanco had freed them from the Count's castle by successfully piloting the Count's flying machine from his tower room.

Antonio shrugged. The sea was home to him. He had no idea what lay in the lands past the coastlines and he didn't want to know. Most land maps had *Here be dragons* written on them in the parts where no one had been because no one knew for certain what they would find there. He was happy to leave it like that.

'Is that the only route to Badakhshan?' he asked.

Gump thought hard for a moment.

'There is a way in from the north,' he said. 'It's very dangerous—lots of slave traders and wild animals and deserts filled with evil spirits—but it is possible.'

'They won't go that way,' said Blanco, aghast at the very thought. 'They'll take the quickest and the easiest route.' He knew the dapper Count would never agree to make such a difficult journey.

Antonio interrupted them. 'Just tell me which direction you want me to go in.'

'East,' said Blanco confidently. 'Head for Acre.'

Antonio gave the order and the pirate ship surged forward.

Azaz was desperately trying to find Blanco's ship. Rameel had finally let Micha go and Azaz had left not long after to tell Blanco about the change in route. But Azaz was having trouble finding the pirate ship. He didn't think they would be this far behind but it was difficult to see through the fog.

When the fog lifted he was horrified to find no ship in sight at all. Sighing, he changed from his southerly direction and headed east towards the Holy Land.

'If we don't find them in Acre,' said Blanco, 'then we're in trouble. This is all your fault—yours and

Magdalena's. If you hadn't made up that stupid rhyme about the adept then the Count and Luca would never have believed that Eva was the only one who could retrieve the heartstone.'

He was sitting in the prow of the ship looking straight ahead, hoping desperately to catch sight of the golden ship.

'It's my fault,' said Gump. 'Don't blame Magdalena.'

'You may have been the one who made up the legend,' said Blanco bitterly, 'but she was the one who betrayed Eva to them in Venice.'

Gump sighed. This was an argument that had been raging since they left. Gump couldn't believe that Magdalena would betray Eva but Blanco was equally sure that she had. He had to believe the evidence of his own eyes. He had seen her go into the golden ship the night before she and Eva were captured. What possible reason could she have had other than to betray Eva? It would hardly have been a social visit. And it couldn't have just been a coincidence that they were kidnapped the very next day.

'We'll find them in Acre,' said Gump, not wanting to have the argument again.

'But what if we don't?'

'Then we'll keep going until we do,' said Gump, with a confidence that he didn't truly feel.

Blanco was frustrated that he had been so close to Eva and yet had failed to save her. He couldn't believe the Count had risked using firepowder on a wooden ship. The whole thing could have gone up in flames. Blanco knew the risks of firepowder even better than the Count did and he would never have dared use it in that way. It was too unpredictable, too dangerous.

Blanco suddenly became aware of a warmth in the air.

'Azaz?' he said, looking up.

Gump looked around expectantly. He wanted to believe in the angels. He would dearly love to see one. He had come across plenty of strange things on his travels, but never an angel and he wasn't about to discount them just because he hadn't actually seen one—at least not until he had definite proof one way or the other.

'Is he here?' he asked Blanco with interest. He could feel, hear, and see nothing.

'I think so. He's trying to tell me something,' said Blanco, closing his eyes in concentration. He didn't find it as easy as Eva did to talk to them. She could see them and talk to them without even thinking about it whereas Blanco really had to concentrate. He had never seen Azaz although sometimes he could see a glowing red light when the angel spoke. He could see such a light now hovering above the dark water.

Eventually he made out what Azaz was saying.

'You're going the wrong way.'

Chapter 2

Constantinople

'Did you find him?' asked Micha. Her golden wings blended perfectly with her surroundings.

She was perched on the top of the Hagia Sophia—the highest and most ornate church in Constantinople. From here she had a perfect view of the city and the harbour. Sparkling golden domes, highly decorated columns, and flat roofs stretched out before her surrounded by the beautiful blue sea. Just before Azaz joined her she had been watching the activity on the golden ship as the crew carried out the preparations for the next stage of the journey into the Black Sea and beyond. She turned to look at Azaz who hovered by her side. His red tunic and dark wings stood out against the blues, whites, and golds of the city.

'I did but I was too late,' said Azaz. 'They'll try to catch up on the route or, if not, to get to Badakhshan first.'

Micha made a face. 'What if they don't? The journey will take months. Anything could happen.'

Azaz nodded. 'I know,' he said. 'But what other choice do we have? All we can do is watch over Eva and hope that Blanco catches us up in time. You know that we can't interfere.'

Micha would have laughed if the situation hadn't been so serious. She was always the one telling Azaz not to *interfere and so it was ironic that now he was warning her. But she knew he was right. It was the strictest of all the rules—that they shouldn't interfere in human affairs. The punishment for it if they were caught was to be returned to the pit. Neither Azaz nor Micha were willing to take that risk. It was becoming more and more difficult but they had to let the story unfold in its own time.*

Eva gazed at the bustling street below. For the first time in weeks, she was looking at a city rather than the sea. And what a city! Eva had already travelled much further than girls of her age—or any age—but she was still amazed by the sights laid out before her here. Every single building looked different from anything she had ever seen before. There were golden domes and intricate carvings and hundreds of little coloured tiles making up beautiful mosaics. The streets were full of strangely dressed people. Even the smells and sounds were different.

Eva had been woken early that morning by the early morning church bells. They were similar to the church bells that tolled at most hours of the day in Venice. But this most definitely was not Venice. She shivered suddenly, feeling very alone. Her angels had disappeared earlier—Azaz to try to find Blanco's ship and Micha to search the city. They had travelled with her for years, ever since she had chanced upon them talking in a church one day. Recently she had begun to wonder whether they had found her deliberately, for surely it couldn't just be a coincidence that she was now caught up in this big adventure.

She leaned out of the window and sniffed and her nostrils were immediately assailed by the hundred and one spices that hung in the air day and night. And by a large amount of dust. She sneezed.

'Bless you,' said a voice from behind her.

Eva turned round.

'I didn't hear you come back in,' she said, in surprise.

Magdalena smiled and put down her basket.

'I wish I could go outside,' said Eva, a little forlornly. She didn't understand why she wasn't allowed to go out with Magdalena. After all, they were both prisoners.

'It's very hot and rather dirty,' said Magdalena, looking down with a sigh at her white dress. It had been pristine when she left Malta a few weeks earlier but was now grubby and looked as though it had recently been used to wash the floor. 'You're better off up here.'

Up here was the top of a tower, part of a house belonging to a friend of Luca Ferron's. It was a luxurious room with velvet seats and golden goblets and plates to eat and drink from but it was still a prison. Eva hated it. She wanted to be outside in the fresh air. Everything looked so exciting out there. She wanted to explore.

'Did you see him?' asked Eva. She never used Luca's name unless she absolutely had to. She shivered at the thought that she had nearly been married to him. Thankfully Blanco had saved her by turning up at the church with a fake marriage certificate claiming that she was already married to him. The Count frightened her too but in a different way. He was volatile— sometimes he would get angry and scream and shout for no reason—but she was much more terrified of Luca Ferron, for she thought he had no soul.

Magdalena shook her head. 'No,' she said. 'I didn't see anyone except the guards.'

'Why do you think they let you go out and not me?'

Magdalena shrugged her shoulders. 'Maybe because they know that I won't try to escape,' she said. 'I'd be too scared.'

'But why should that be any different for me?' asked Eva plaintively. 'I'm in a strange country. What chance do I have of escaping?'

Magdalena raised a quizzical eyebrow. 'Your angels?' she said.

It was Eva's turn to shrug. She hadn't seen Azaz since he had gone to find Blanco's ship; she hoped he had reached them in time.

'Blanco will save us anyway,' she said hopefully. 'I don't need to run away. They nearly caught up with us on the ship so they can't be that far behind. They might even be here now.'

Eva had been heartbroken when the sea fog had lifted and the pirate ship had disappeared but she had quickly recovered. After all the adventures and journeys that she and Blanco had shared, he wouldn't leave her in danger now.

'We did change direction to lose them,' said Magdalena. 'That's why we're in Constantinople instead of Acre.'

'But I sent Azaz to tell them,' said Eva.

'He might not have been in time,' replied Magdalena. 'I'm just saying, don't get your hopes up, my dear. We may have a long journey ahead of us.'

'At least he's following us,' said Eva. 'At least he knows where we're heading. At some point, he'll find us, I know he will. Long before we get *there*.' Eva never referred to the Blue Mountain by name, either.

Magdalena looked at her thoughtfully. 'What if he doesn't?' she asked. 'Have you thought what will happen?'

Eva wasn't listening any more. She had caught sight of Azaz and Micha flying outside the window. She ran over and leant out.

'Isn't it a beautiful city?' she said, spreading her arms out wide. 'Why are people scared to visit new places when they're as beautiful as this? I can't wait to show Blanco.'

Micha smiled at Eva's enthusiasm although her smile faded before it reached her eyes. Azaz flew down and took Eva's hands in his and gazed at her. Eva's smile faltered at the grave look on his face.

'Eva,' he said. 'I was too late. Blanco isn't coming here.'

'Of course he is,' she said, her bottom lip trembling slightly. 'Where else would he go?'

'I was too late,' said Azaz. 'They were too far behind. They've gone to the Holy Land. They'll try and catch you up on the way.'

Eva stared at him in horror. 'But what if they don't?' she whispered in terrified tones. 'What if they don't? The Count and Luca Ferron are going to kill me! I know they are!'

She wrenched her hands from his and, turning, threw herself down on the bed and started to cry.

★ ★ ★

They had only arrived that afternoon and already Antonio was preparing to leave again. After Azaz's message they had had to decide whether to follow the other ship north or continue on their original route.

'We're already a few days behind,' Antonio had pointed out. 'By the time we turn round, go back, and then head north, they'll be almost a week ahead of you. If you stick to the original plan, then you might be able to catch them up en route.'

'But they'll be following a different one,' said Blanco in frustration. He couldn't believe how close they had been, only to be miles apart again. 'They'll be much further north.'

'There are meeting points on the way,' said Gump. 'Lots of places where the routes converge. There's not just one Silk Road, you know, there are several. We could catch up with them on the way.'

'And if we don't?' asked Blanco gloomily. After all, they hadn't had much luck so far. He didn't trust Count Maleficio or Luca Ferron. He knew how much they wanted the heartstone. They both believed that it would bring them great power, although Blanco wasn't entirely sure how. Blanco knew that they were convinced that Eva was the key to what they desired, because he had read the Count's diary, in which Eva was referred to as the sacrifice. At least this meant that she was probably safe until the Blue Mountain. But Blanco was determined to stop them from getting that far. He was going to save Eva.

'At least we know where they're heading,' said

Gump. 'We'll get there before them. Our way is much quicker.'

Antonio had been right. Acre was in ruins. They had docked there, at the old harbour, but there had been nothing but crumbling houses and shattered walls. It was hard to believe that it had once been a busy, bustling port, full of merchants and crusaders. They had quickly boarded the ship again and Antonio had dropped them off at a port to the north. He stayed only long enough to do that, not wanting even to spend a night there. He wanted to get back to known waters.

'You don't want to come with us, do you?' Blanco had asked him hopefully. Antonio was strong and a wonderful fighter. It would be good to have someone like him on the journey with them. There would be lots of danger ahead.

'Sorry,' said Antonio, shivering with distaste, 'but I'm a sea-dog right down to the marrow of my bones. Cut me and seawater would run out instead of blood. I'm no use to anyone on dry land.'

Blanco thought that he was the same but in reverse. He spent his entire time on board ships fighting seasickness. He was happy to be on dry land again.

Blanco couldn't quite believe where he was. It was a dream for many boys of his age to sail to the Holy Land and try to reach Jerusalem. He had been brought up on tales of Crusaders and knights and now he was actually here. Only they weren't heading for Jerusalem. That lay in the opposite direction. They were heading into the desert and far beyond.

Although excited, he couldn't help but feel a little frightened about what lay ahead. But his great-uncle Marco Polo had travelled this way before and had survived.

Blanco looked around him. He and Gump were sitting in the middle of a caravanserai, a resting place for travelling merchants and pilgrims. He was surrounded by men from many different countries. The air was thick with smoke from the pipes the men were puffing and the vast cooking fires dotted around. Behind them were stables for the horses and some other fully laden, strange looking beasts in the corner. Had he been less tired Blanco might have been worried by the weird assortment of men and beasts but, as it was, he was too weary even to think, never mind worry. Blanco couldn't make out one conversation that he could actually understand. Everyone was speaking in languages completely unknown to him. He could tell, though, that all sorts of deals were being done as goods were being exchanged, hands shaken, and hugs shared. It was disconcerting but a little part of him loved it—the thought of new countries, new people, and adventures ahead.

As he lay there, in the strange courtyard, surrounded by foreign sounds, smells, and sights, he tried to think about something comforting.

'At least we've done a fair portion of the journey,' he said to Gump.

Gump looked at him incredulously. 'No, we haven't,' he said. 'We haven't even started. Tomorrow is when the journey really begins.'

★ ★ ★

In the morning, after a sleep filled with strange dreams, Blanco woke to find that Gump had disappeared and Blanco was surrounded by the chaos of the caravanserai.

A man completely covered in furs, one of which still had the head of an animal attached, bumped into him, almost knocking him over. Blanco began to protest but his voice died away as he saw that the man had a large sword slung at his side. He swallowed his anger and said nothing. The man also wore a large fur hat. Blanco watched him walk away, wondering how he didn't melt. A lot of the men were dressed in long white shirts and baggy trousers which looked deliciously cool. Blanco thought that he might buy some for himself.

He was nudged in the back again and he turned round determined to stand his ground this time. He found himself facing a camel. At least he was fairly sure that was what it was. It looked a bit like a horse but was much larger and had a hump on its back. Its hair was coarse and thick and its long face and big teeth gave it a friendly appearance. It was kneeling down—and Blanco had never seen a horse do that—for loading. Whole rugs and panniers full of precious stones were being secured to its back, as well as bags of corn and other foodstuffs.

Blanco could see Gump returning, making his way through the crowds with ease. He looked perfectly at home. He had somehow managed to adapt his clothes so that they looked much more loose fitting and cool while Blanco looked completely out of place in his bright blue Venetian outfit. Gump's face was relaxed and he looked twenty years younger. Travel obviously agreed with him. If only his family could see him now.

Blanco's father had always doubted that Gump had really travelled to all the places that he said he had. But if he saw Gump now then surely he would believe him. And maybe he would be proud of his only son too. Just because Blanco had never wanted to go into the family business didn't mean that he was a bad son. He just liked different things from the rest of his family.

Blanco noticed that Gump wasn't alone.

'What is that—a camel?' asked Blanco.

'Not what,' said Gump, patting the beast on its rump. 'Who. This is Safira.'

'I thought we were travelling on horses!'

'No, no. Camels are what we need. We might get some horses when we get to Damascus but camels are the best way for now. They can carry more, they need less to drink, and are better suited to travelling through the desert.'

Blanco looked unsure but his uncle had done this before. He knew what he was talking about. He watched as Gump tied the camel up. When he had finished he sat by the fire, pulled out a map, and motioned for Blanco to sit beside him.

'This is where we're going,' he said. He pulled out a small, sharp knife and used it to trace the route. 'We're here in Tyre. We'll travel to Damascus and then cross the desert to Baghdad. Then up over the mountains.'

'And Eva?' demanded Blanco. 'Which way will she go?' He was daunted by the length of the journey they had to complete. He and Gump had gone over the route before they left Venice but now that they had actually started, Blanco was getting a firmer idea of the distances involved—and they were much larger than he had first thought.

Gump tapped his knife against his chin for a moment as he perused the map.

'This is where they would have headed north,' he said. 'They would have headed for Constantinople. That means they would probably continue sailing down along the Black Sea and then cross this piece of land and then across the Caspian Sea. It means they have to cross the Karakum desert.' Here he stopped and Blanco was quick to pounce on his hesitation.

'What?' he said. 'What's wrong with the desert?'

'It's much worse than the one we have to cross,' said Gump. 'But I'm sure they know what they're doing.'

Blanco wasn't so sure. Neither the Count nor Luca Ferron were natural travellers. They both liked their little luxuries too much for that.

'You have to remember,' said Gump. 'They *need* Eva to get to the Blue Mountain alive. They'll look after her.'

Blanco nodded but he didn't look very reassured.

'Then they'll head south and into Badakhshan from the north. We'll be coming from the west.'

Blanco nodded. Both journeys looked much the same distance but Gump was adamant that their way would be quicker.

'Now,' said Gump, 'as you can see, we are about to set off on a very long journey.'

Blanco rolled his eyes. His great-uncle, like most adults, had a bad habit of stating the obvious.

'Don't roll your eyes at me, boy,' said Gump. 'I'm being serious. This isn't a game, you know. This is a dangerous business.'

Blanco leaned forward. 'I'm very well aware of that,' he said through gritted teeth. 'Maybe more than you. It was your stupid game that set all this in motion, if you remember.'

Gump blushed at this. If he hadn't sent coded letters to Magdalena twenty years ago telling the legend of the heartstone, then none of this might have happened. Count Maleficio would never have tried to decode the letters, he would never have joined forces with Luca Ferron, and together they would never have captured Eva and gone off in search of the heartstone.

'And it's your girlfriend who has got Eva into all this trouble,' he continued.

Gump frowned.

'Now this is what I want to talk about,' he said. 'This journey we're heading into, it's a difficult one. Very dangerous.'

Blanco opened his mouth to interrupt.

'Now don't try and tell me that you know all about dangerous journeys. The ones you've been on so far have been mere child's play compared to this one. I know, I know. Wolves and bandits and pirates and things. I've heard your tales, remember. And, believe me, they are nothing, nothing at all, compared to what you'll have to face in the coming weeks.'

'So . . . '

'So,' continued Gump. 'We should start as we mean to go on. No blame. No fights. No arguments. Say what you want to say here and now and then nothing more is to be said about it. We have to go on this journey as friends or we're never going to survive. So, go on, say it.'

Blanco remained silent.

'Well?'

'Oh, I'm allowed to speak now, am I?' said Blanco.

'Only you weren't letting me say anything a moment ago.' He glared at his uncle. 'If we're not going to argue then you have to believe me when I say that I saw Magdalena going into the ship the night before they were taken and so she must have betrayed Eva.'

'What I will believe,' said Gump in measured tones, 'is that you think you saw her going up the gangplank.'

Blanco started to protest but Gump held up a silencing hand. 'And I believe that you really believe that. But I have known Magdalena a lot longer than you have and I can't believe she has changed so much that she would betray a young girl. So, since we're never going to agree, maybe we should agree to disagree, at least until we all meet up again and find out what really happened.'

Blanco nodded grudgingly. He knew he was right and Gump would find that out when they met up with the others. He didn't want to fight any more.

'Anything else you want to bring up now?' asked Gump.

'One thing,' said Blanco. 'Will we get there first?'

Gump rubbed his eyebrows, a sign that he was worried.

'I just don't know,' he said eventually. 'I think so. I hope so.'

'We have to,' said Blanco firmly. 'No matter how difficult the journey is we have to get there first.'

'We have to move fast anyway,' said Gump. 'We must reach there before winter comes. We don't want to be stuck in those mountains when winter sets in. Nobody could survive that.'

'No,' said Blanco, 'you don't understand. If we don't get there first, then Eva might die.'

Chapter 3

Constantinople

Eva took a deep breath and immediately sneezed.

She looked round the bustling crowds and drew back slightly against the wall. After being enclosed in a ship and then in a room it all suddenly seemed a little too much. There was so much noise, so many things to look at, so much colour, so many people. It was amazing, wonderful, and utterly terrifying all at the same time. Constantinople was so different from anywhere she had ever been before. Not just the buildings but the people. Eva was amazed by it all.

'Now don't look about too much, my dear,' said Magdalena. 'You don't want to draw attention to yourself.'

Eva looked at Magdalena's bowed head in astonishment. Not look about? What was the point of being in a new place just to ignore it? But she said nothing. After all, if Magdalena was never going to look up then she would have no idea what Eva was doing. She looked behind them at the two huge guards that Luca Ferron had insisted should accompany them. Luca and the Count had finally decided that she could be allowed out when they heard that Blanco was still heading for Acre. The dark angel, Rameel, had overheard Azaz tell Eva and he had passed the news on.

Count Maleficio had barely been able to contain his glee.

'I knew it,' he had gloated. 'And it's all down to me. You have to admit it, Ferron. It was my decision to fire the beast. And I was the one who said we should change direction.'

Luca Ferron had smiled at him although Eva could tell that he was only humouring the Count. Since the journey began Count Maleficio had been getting more and more pleased with himself. He had Magdalena, the love of his life. He had Eva, the adept who would retrieve the heartstone for them. And, most importantly at the moment, he had managed to lose Blanco and Marco Polo, the two people he hated most in the world. He thought it was all because of his planning, but Eva had long ago worked out that it was Luca Ferron who was in charge of this operation, although he was careful to let the Count think that they were equal partners. Eva could see that there was going to be trouble on the journey ahead if the Count ever realized that.

At the moment though, the only blessing that came from Blanco not following them was that she was allowed to go outside with Magdalena, albeit with the guards watching their every move.

'It's for your own protection,' Luca had said.

Eva wasn't convinced. They looked much more like gaolers than protectors but she knew she had little choice in the matter. But here she was at last, right in the middle of the bustling street that she had been watching from her window. Everywhere she looked she saw something new. The market stalls were piled high with spices and pottery and food. The stall to her left was like a living palette of colour with bowls of orange saffron, yellow turmeric, and red chillies. The noise was incessant and everything looked exciting. The overall feeling was of a city constantly in motion—a place where east and west met—and passed through. Eva knew that she was on the threshold of a whole new world. If only Blanco had been here with her she would have loved it even more. She wished she had some way of capturing it in a picture and sharing it with him.

A shout to her left caught her attention—and that of the guards. Two carts had collided and one had overturned. A basket of oranges had fallen into the dirt. The two drivers were arguing over whose fault it was, while others were scrabbling for the fruit. The argument escalated, punches were thrown, and soon a full-scale fight had broken out.

Magdalena was closely inspecting some cloth, with the thought of buying some to replace their hideously dirty clothes, when Eva grabbed her and pulled her along the street.

'What are you doing?'

'Ssssh!' hissed Eva. 'Come on. Follow me!'

The eagle-eyed Eva had spotted that their two gaolers were engrossed in watching the fight. She dragged a protesting Magdalena across the street and into a small shop whose owner was out cheering on the fighters.

'What are you doing?' asked Magdalena again. 'Where are we going?'

'Anywhere,' said Eva. 'Back to the docks, maybe. I'm sure we'll be able to find a ship there.'

'But we have no money,' said Magdalena. 'And you promised you wouldn't try to escape!'

'I don't count it as a promise when it was made to someone who wants to kill me! Anyway, I had my fingers crossed.'

Magdalena wasn't sure how to reply to that.

'We can head to Acre,' said Eva. She had been thinking about this while trapped in the upper room. If Blanco was still heading to Acre then she might be able to meet him there. 'We'll find a way.'

'A way where?' queried a smooth voice. 'You're not trying to leave us, are you?'

Standing in front of them was a seven-foot angel whose indigo wings were trailing on the ground in front of him. Eva had to strongly resist the urge to stamp on them. As though guessing her intentions Rameel began to hover slightly. He smiled smugly and she glowered at him.

'Why, you've only just arrived,' he said mockingly. 'We couldn't possibly let you leave now. That would just be plain rude. Not when there's still so much of the world to see.'

'Eva?' asked Magdalena with some confusion. Moments before, Eva had been dragging her and rushing through the shop and now she was standing stock still gazing into thin air.

'It's no use,' said Eva, turning to face her. 'You're right. There's nowhere we can go. Let's just go back.'

'Excellent decision,' said Rameel. 'And if you're lucky, I won't tell on you.'

Eva glanced back at him in horror but he merely smiled at her. She had no idea whether he would tell or not. Rameel only ever pleased himself.

Damascus–Baghdad

Blanco looked behind him one last time at the trail of people all accompanied by donkeys, camels, horses, and carts laden with goods of every description. The caravan stretched back into the horizon and he couldn't see the end of it.

He and Gump had joined the pilgrim trail in Damascus where they had bought all their provisions and their horses. Despite their promise not to quarrel on the journey this had been broken almost immediately.

Blanco had fallen in love with a beautiful brown horse with a large star on her forehead and white socks. He thought she was the most perfect horse that he had ever seen, but Gump wasn't sure she was strong enough for the journey.

'Blanco,' he said, 'we're travelling through rough terrain, over mountains and deserts, not trotting along some road outside Venice. This is the sort of horse you need.'

He waved his hand at a big brute of a horse which snarled and snapped his teeth as Blanco took a step closer.

'Maybe not,' said Blanco. 'Why don't you take that one?'

'No, I've picked mine,' said Gump, patting the nose of a docile and rather boring-looking horse. 'Strong, sturdy, reliable. That's what you need.'

'I want this one,' maintained Blanco stubbornly.

Gump sighed. 'If you take this one, and she's too skittish and won't go up hills then I don't want to hear you moaning about it.'

Blanco nodded his agreement and Gump paid for the horses. They then had to buy the rest of the provisions for such a long journey. Blanco was impressed by the way his great-uncle bartered and bargained for all their goods. He was also amazed at just how much they needed. For the first time it struck him that they were heading into areas where there might be no food or water.

For the first part of their journey they had decided to join a pilgrim train going to Baghdad. Travelling in a large group was by far the safest way to cross the desert and mountains, where there were fierce bandits and food and drink could be scarce. By joining their resources together, a group was stronger than if they had all been travelling individually.

'Are you ready?' Gump asked.

'This is it,' said Blanco. 'This is really it. There's no turning back now.'

'You're sure you want to go?'

Blanco looked at him incredulously. Of course he was sure. He couldn't leave Eva in the hands of Count Maleficio and Luca Ferron.

'Of course,' he said. His heart leapt as he said the words. He was terrified and excited at the same time.

'Then let's go,' said Gump and he rode his horse into the pilgrim train. He pulled the camel on a rein behind him. Blanco's horse refused to get in line and so Blanco rode alongside. He didn't mind that. He didn't like to feel hemmed in. As the great train set off he wondered where Eva was. He hadn't heard from Azaz since he had found them on the ship. His only thought was to try to catch up with Eva or to make sure they reached Badakhshan before her.

The Black Sea

Magdalena clutched her blanket tightly round her and tucked herself into a sheltered nook on the deck of the ship. From there she could watch the sailors do their work. It was difficult work because the wind was strong; Magdalena wondered if it would develop into a full blown storm. The ship hugged the coastline, for the middle of the Black Sea was full of squalls and great winds and wasn't easy to sail through. It took longer but it was safer. Looking at the height of the waves, Magdalena wondered just how much worse it could get—and hoped that they wouldn't find out. They had been travelling for three days already and the chill had crept to her bones and settled there. Her clothes were permanently damp and her feet had been frozen for days.

She looked up with a smile on her face as a shadow fell across her, expecting to see Eva. But it was the Count who was standing there. Her smile faded.

'Go away,' she said. 'I have nothing to say to you.'

'But I want to talk to you,' he said, sounding like a petulant child. He squatted down beside her. His cloak billowed out around him making him resemble a bloated silver frog.

She sighed and moved over slightly so that he could squeeze in beside her. At least he gave her some protection against the wind. He sat there for a while, saying nothing.

'Well?' asked Magdalena eventually. 'What is it?'

The Count shifted uncomfortably but still said nothing.

'Have you come to apologize for kidnapping us?' she asked. 'Have you come to say that you're going to set us free when we reach land?'

'I didn't kidnap you!' protested the Count. 'You came . . . '

Magdalena cut him off with a motion of her hand before he could finish the sentence.

'Are you going to let us go?'

The Count shook his head and stared beseechingly at her with his strange silver-grey eyes.

'Magdalena,' he said, 'can't you love me?'

Magdalena sighed loudly. The Count asked her this on average about three times a day. He seemed to think he could wear her down by repeating it over and over again.

'No, Christobal,' she said firmly.

'Don't call me that. My name's Maleficio.'

'Well, it's a stupid name.'

'I've loved you for twenty years. I'm doing all this for you. I'd do anything for you.'

Magdalena knew this was true. He had built her a convent in Malta and arranged to have her installed as abbess without telling her. He was searching for the heartstone for her, without her wanting him to. There was one thing that she did want from him, however.

'If you'd do anything for me,' she said, 'then let Eva go.'

'No,' he said immediately. 'I can't do that.'

'Why not?'

'She's the only one who can get what we want. She's the adept. She can get the heartstone out.'

'Christobal, it's just a legend,' sighed Magdalena. She also said this every day but she might as well have been talking to herself for the Count paid no attention to her words. But she kept trying in the hope that one day he would believe her. 'The heartstone has no magical properties. It's just a stone. If it even exists. What do you think it can do?'

His silver-grey eyes stared at her with a glint of obsession.

'It's the philosopher's stone,' he said. 'It will turn metal into gold. It holds the secret to eternal life. Just think, once I have turned it into a potion, we can live together for ever. It will make you love me. It'll just be you and me—for ever.'

Magdalena couldn't contain a shiver of disgust at the thought. She didn't want to live for ever, and certainly not with Count Maleficio.

'It's a stone! It's just a stone. And I will never love you. Not even if I live for centuries! And I have no wish to live for ever.'

The Count clearly didn't believe her.

'Everyone wants to live for ever,' he said.

'Is that why Luca wants it as well?'

'Of course,' he said, although he frowned as he said it.

'You don't sound very sure,' she said.

'I don't know what he wants it for,' admitted the Count. 'We have agreed to halve it when we get it. What he does with his half is up to him.'

'You really believe he will give you half?' asked Magdalena.

The Count looked surprised. 'It's not his to give,' he said. 'You may as well ask whether I will give him half?'

Magdalena hid a little smile. Like Eva, she had noticed that it was Luca Ferron who was really in charge. She wasn't sure the Count would ever get his half of the stone.

'What if I don't want to live for ever?' she asked, going back to their original conversation.

The Count stood up and smiled coldly down at her.

'You don't have a choice,' he said and walked away, leaving Magdalena even more chilled than before.

Rameel was sitting on the rails, listening to the conversation. He was laughing as the Count stormed off. A moment later he was falling as a hand tugged hard on his wings. The suddenness of the fall meant that he almost tumbled into the sea before his wings started working. He only just saved himself from crashing into the waves.

'You shouldn't listen to other people's conversations,' said Azaz flying above him.

Rameel glowered at him.

'You nearly got my wings wet,' he said crossly. 'And you know how long they take to dry. Where have you been, anyway? I haven't seen you for days.'

'Just around,' said Azaz. 'Keeping out of your master's way.'

'He's not my master!' spat out Rameel. 'I'm no one's servant.'

'Really? Then why are you here?' asked Azaz conversationally. 'What's your interest in the heartstone? You don't need eternal life. You've already got that. And you don't need gold.'

A flicker of fear flashed briefly across Rameel's face but then he laughed.

'I'm just having fun,' he said. 'You know how I like to play with these humans. It's all a game. Our game. And may the best angel win.'

With that he flew off, leaving Azaz staring thoughtfully after him. Rameel had fallen because he liked to teach humans destructive ways for fun. It sounded as though, despite having spent millennia in the pit, he still hadn't learned his lesson.

'I hear you wanted to leave us,' said Luca Ferron.

Eva glared at him. She had hoped that Rameel hadn't told Luca about her attempt to escape in Constantinople. Nothing had been said while they were still there but now that they were on a ship on the Black Sea and there really was no hope of running away, Luca had called her into his cabin.

Eva said nothing.

'If you try to escape again I'll put you and Magdalena in chains for the rest of the journey,' he said calmly.

Eva gazed at him in horror. She had no doubt he meant what he said. He was still smiling but she knew that meant nothing. His eyes were cold and hard and merciless. He was clearly waiting for a reply.

'I won't,' she said eventually, shrugging her shoulders. 'Where would I go? We're too far from home now. I'd be a fool to run away.'

As she said it she knew it was true. Despair settled on her. She *was* too far from home now and she

didn't know where Blanco was. She knew that they had changed course after the pirate ship had almost caught up with them, so Blanco could be anywhere. Even if he had gone to Acre he would have left there by now.

'And know this,' said Luca, leaning forward, his smile vanishing, making his cheeks look too big for his face. 'I will always catch you. Rameel will always find you and tell me.'

Eva tried not to meet his eyes, terrified of what she would find there. This man scared her much more than the Count. Magdalena could always protect her from Count Maleficio but no one, not even the angels, could protect her from Luca Ferron. He seemed to thrive on her look of fear for he smiled again and sat back.

'It doesn't have to be a difficult journey,' he said. The door opened behind him but he didn't notice. 'You know I can't kill you because I need you. But if you make things difficult then I may decide to kill Magdalena. She's no use to me whatsoever.'

'What?' asked the Count, pushing the door open wider. 'How dare you? How dare you threaten to kill Magdalena?'

Luca whirled round to find his colleague standing there. Eva looked from one to the other. The Count towered over the smaller man but Eva could tell that Luca Ferron wasn't scared at all. But the Count wasn't scared of Luca either and appeared equally determined to get what he wanted. They both seemed to have forgotten that she was still sitting there.

'This isn't just your venture, Ferron,' said the Count. 'We're in this together.'

Luca laughed—a very unpleasant laugh. 'Of course we are,' he said soothingly. 'Until the end. Until the sacrifice. And then it's each man for himself.'

The Count picked up a goblet and raised it to Luca.

'And may the best man win,' he said.

As they argued, Eva took her chance and crept out of the door, trying to ignore the word 'sacrifice' which continued to echo in her head. She had always known that the Count and Luca Ferron needed her. She had never truly accepted until that moment that she might die in the process.

Chapter 4

---❦ ❦---

Mount Ararat

Mount Ararat was like a talisman in the distance beckoning them forward. It had been in sight for three days yet it was only now that they were finally approaching its lower reaches.

'Do you think the Ark's still up there?' asked Eva.

Magdalena shook her head. 'I have no idea,' she replied. 'It's impossible to climb up, for the snow on the top never melts and so every year more and more is added.'

'It would be completely buried then,' said Eva.

Magdalena nodded in agreement.

Mount Ararat was where Noah's Ark was supposed to have come to rest after the Great Flood. It stood out from all the surrounding mountains, like a giant hook. Eva was sure that the Ark was still up there.

Eva had been fascinated by everything she'd seen since they had reached dry land again. She hadn't been sorry to leave the ship, where she had felt confined and trapped. Now, in the open air, she felt much better and more hopeful about everything. Blanco could catch up at any moment. Meanwhile she was determined to enjoy all the different lands they were travelling through. How many people, she thought, got a chance to see this much of the world? She might have been forced on this journey but that was no reason not to enjoy it while it happened. She could worry about the heartstone when they got to Badakhshan. Although she was sure that Blanco would have caught up with them long before then.

'I bet Azaz would know,' said Eva. 'And even if he doesn't he could fly up and find out.'

'Not if it's covered in snow,' said Magdalena.

'Oh, yes,' said Eva, a little disappointed. Then she brightened. 'Who would ever have thought that we would travel so far? Everyone is going to be so jealous when I go back and tell them what I've seen. I might even write a book about it all, like Blanco's great-uncle.'

Given that Blanco had taught Eva to read only a few months ago this was a rather ambitious undertaking. Magdalena looked at her thoughtfully. Since they had left the ship Eva had refused to talk about the dangers that might lie ahead. She was pretending that they were on a fantastic journey and that Blanco would be there, waiting for them, at the end. Magdalena knew that was unlikely to happen and thought that Eva should start thinking about what might happen to her. But whenever Magdalena mentioned Badakhshan or the heartstone Eva just laughed and said that Blanco would save her.

The angels were circling the mountain summit, checking the route ahead.

'I have to go and find Blanco,' said Azaz.

'I know,' said Micha, although she didn't want him to go. She didn't like being left alone with Rameel. He didn't scare her—she was just as powerful as he was—but he made her feel uncomfortable. He made her doubt herself and he did like to play games. Micha liked things to be straightforward. Azaz and Rameel never tired of taunting each other and testing each other but she didn't like to join in. They had both fallen because they liked to interfere, although for very different reasons. Azaz interfered because he loved to teach new things while Rameel interfered only to cause destruction. She was different. She had chosen to fall because she was in love with a human and the only way she could be with him was to take human form for the span of his life before turning into an angel again. But Rameel always made her feel uncomfortable about all that.

Azaz knew what she was thinking.

'Maybe this time you should ask him a few questions,' he said. 'Ask him about why he fell. He might tell you something when I'm not around. He's got a secret. And not just from us. From Luca and the Count. He's after the heartstone as well, I'm sure of it.'

Micha nodded. Rameel was acting even more erratically than usual. Sometimes he would hover over Eva almost protectively. Other times he would disappear, sometimes for days.

'There are times,' she said, 'when I wish I could just fly ahead and take the stone myself.'

Azaz looked surprised. It wasn't like Micha to want to interfere.

'But you wouldn't be able to,' he said. 'You know we can't go underground. That's the one thing stopping Rameel from flying there himself.'

'I know,' said Micha. 'It's just a wish. How will you find Blanco?'

'I know the route they were planning to take,' said Azaz, 'so I'll follow that and hope that I can find them quickly.'

'And how will you find us again?'

Azaz smiled at her. 'You know I can always find you, Micha,' he said. 'But I'll aim to meet you on the other side of the Caspian Sea.'

Micha nodded. She would miss him but they had to know that Blanco was safe and find out if his path was destined to cross Eva's before they reached Badakhshan.

'Men with dog heads.'

'No, no, men with tails.'

Eva and Magdalena were whispering outlandish tales to each other. They were laughing but it was partly to keep away their fears. Neither of them really knew what they would find beyond the mountains and they were scared.

'I don't believe any of the stories,' said Eva defiantly. 'We may all dress differently or eat different food or pray at different times but so far there's been nothing *really* different about anyone that we've met. I don't believe all these stories.'

She didn't say that nothing would ever be as frightening as Luca Ferron but she was thinking it.

'What, not even the one about the men who have one big foot which they use to cover themselves from the sun,' teased Magdalena. 'You said that was in Marco's book.'

Eva giggled at what they must look like. 'There must

be some other explanation,' she said. 'I can believe in unicorns because there are so many stories about them that they must exist. But men with huge feet which can cover their heads or noses which hang down to the ground. No. I can't believe those stories are true.'

'Are you calling Marco Polo a liar?' teased Magdalena, for she knew that Eva was in awe of Blanco's great-uncle.

'Of course not,' said Eva quickly. 'But he travelled much much further than us. Maybe such things do exist in other countries. Just not the ones we've been to. I'll ask him when I see him.'

'Well,' said Magdalena as she looked ahead at yet another mountain pass. 'We might be about to find out for ourselves.'

'What I really want to find,' moaned Eva, 'is a soft feather bed.' Her bones were aching. She had never had to ride as much in her life. Day after day on a horse had left her bruised and aching. Every morning when she climbed back on she wanted to cry with the pain but she was given no choice. They all felt the same but greed and fear were driving the Count and Luca Ferron on. They were determined to reach Badakhshan before Blanco.

Shifting uncomfortably on her horse, Magdalena could only sigh in agreement.

Damascus–Baghdad

Blanco couldn't take his eyes off the splendour of the night-time camel train. Even though the same thing happened every night he was still mesmerized by it. After stopping for evening prayers—the fifth prayer stop of the day—big torches would be lit all along the procession and the train would continue for a few hours. The torches stretched far ahead into the darkness, blazing a trail through the night in the same way that the stars lit up the sky.

It had been a long and tedious journey so far. The heat and dust of the desert swirled around them every day, draining them of both their energy and sight. Blanco was glad they were part of the pilgrim train for he couldn't believe they would ever have found their way through the desert otherwise. Every day they seemed to plough the same path, through the same dunes, always heading towards the same horizon. They never seemed to reach anywhere different, but he had to believe that one day they would arrive in Baghdad. They had been caught in a sandstorm the night before. It had been ferocious and petrifying. The whole train had come to a standstill and everyone had taken shelter in their covered carts. This morning the storm had finally abated and they had climbed out, only to discover huge sand drifts piled up against the sides of the carts, some of which were completely covered. The sand had forced its way inside the wagon and Blanco was still picking it out of his eyes, his teeth, and anywhere else it had lodged itself.

But there was no sign of a storm now. As the torch-lit procession continued Gump climbed into their covered wagon determined to get some sleep. Blanco loved to walk for a while at night, watching the stars and the torches mirror each other. The caravan, which could be so noisy during the day, fell silent about now and he could sink into his own thoughts. He usually spent this time thinking of Eva and working out ways of rescuing her. He was lost in such thoughts when a voice spoke out of the darkness.

'Marco Polo?'

Blanco jumped and peered into the night. He could see a man with a scarf tied around his head and shoulders in the local style. The loose cloth was pulled across his mouth to keep the sand out; all Blanco could see were his eyes. He seemed to be an old man, about the same age as Gump.

'He's my great-uncle,' he said. 'He's resting. Can I help?'

'Not unless you've got forty dinar to give me.'

Blanco looked at him in astonishment. That was an enormous sum of money! How could his great-uncle have run up such a debt in just a few days? And on what? They had bought everything they needed for the journey in Damascus and Blanco had seen the money handed over then. So what could this man be talking about?

'Are you sure you're looking for the right man?' he asked.

'Oh yes,' the man replied grimly. 'And I've been looking for a long time. Marco! Come out!'

'What's all the noise?' came a grumpy voice from inside the covered wagon. 'Can't an old man get any sleep?'

Gump stuck his head out of the opening and glared at Blanco. He knew someone else was there but he couldn't see him properly.

'Can't your business wait till morning?' he asked the stranger.

'Why?' came the reply as the man stepped forward into the torchlight. 'So you can run off again without paying your debts? I've waited forty years, Polo. I'm not waiting any longer.'

Gump peered further into the darkness but he still couldn't see anything, although he thought the voice was vaguely familiar. He pulled out the glass roundels that he sometimes wore to help him to see better. Putting them on he looked again.

'Good lord!' he exclaimed. 'Mahmut! I never thought I'd see you again!'

'Thought or hoped?' replied Mahmut.

'My dear man . . . ' started Gump.

'Don't try and charm me,' said Mahmut. 'I want my forty dinar and I want them now.'

'It was never that much,' said Gump.

'It was forty years ago,' replied Mahmut. 'Maybe you've forgotten how much it really was.'

Blanco had been watching this exchange with bemusement.

'What's going on?' he asked.

'Mahmut,' said Gump, clambering down from the wagon. 'This is my great-nephew, Blanco.'

Mahmut bowed and after a moment's hesitation Blanco bowed back.

'I owe him some money,' said Gump.

'So I gather,' said Blanco. 'But we don't have much left. Certainly not forty dinar.'

'You're just like your great-uncle!' exclaimed Mahmut. 'That was what he said last time and then he went off to get some and I never saw him again! I searched for you for days and couldn't find you.'

'Well, you've found me now,' said Gump climbing down from the wagon.

Blanco helped his great-uncle down. He wasn't sure if the two old men were about to start fighting and so he stood between them. Gump pushed him aside and grabbed Mahmut. Then, to Blanco's surprise, they started laughing and hugging each other.

'Forty dinar!' choked out Gump.

'Well, it was worth a try,' laughed Mahmut.

Blanco was thoroughly confused but it certainly didn't look as though they were about to start fighting. He turned back towards the cart.

It was at that moment the bandits attacked.

They came out of nowhere. A whole group of screaming men swinging scimitars. They were dressed head to foot in black swirling robes which allowed them to materialize out of the darkness and then fade back into the night without anyone being able to see them properly. It was hard to tell how many of them there were. There were screams echoing all the way along the pilgrim train.

Mahmut was struck over the head and collapsed in a heap at Gump's feet. As Blanco bent down to check on him he felt the whirr of cold steel pass just above his head and he heard Gump cry out. Blanco collapsed on top of Mahmut. Looking up he saw staring eyes and felt rather than saw the downward swing of steel. Instinctively he rolled to one side and the blade struck the sand. Blanco leapt to his feet desperately searching for a weapon or something—anything—to use in defence.

Gump, who had leapt back at the first scream, now ran forward shouting, a sword in his hand. The threat was enough to cause their attacker to veer off, in search of easier prey. Most people had been sleeping or resting in their wagons and were still befuddled by the sudden onslaught.

'Blanco!' cried a fearful Gump. 'Are you hurt?'

'I'm fine,' said Blanco. 'He missed me.'

Gump went to hug him but Blanco held him off.

'Check Mahmut,' he said curtly. 'And give me the sword!'

'You should stay here,' said Gump. 'You're just a boy.'

Blanco bristled at that.

'I think you forget how long I've been away,' he said. 'I'm not a boy any more. I've seen more than my share of fights in the last few months and I know it's better to join in than cower away in the darkness.'

'I didn't mean anything by it,' protested Gump. 'I just worry about you.'

'Well, don't,' said Blanco, reaching into the wagon and pulling out his sword. 'You stay here and look after Mahmut. You're an old man.'

'Not too old to give you a clip around the ear,' shouted Gump at Blanco's retreating back. Gump closed his eyes. When had this happened? When had Blanco become the fighter and he the one left behind? It didn't feel right. Sighing, he knelt down and searched Mahmut for signs of life, thanking the saints when he found some. He was just about to stand up again when he felt a line of cold steel across the back of his neck.

'Give me your jewels,' a voice said.

'I don't have any,' replied Gump calmly. He spread his palms to emphasize what he was saying, to show that he had nothing of any worth.

The man obviously didn't believe him and dragged Gump towards the wagon, still with the scimitar against his neck. Gump was convinced that his last moments had come. He closed his eyes and started praying, then he felt the metal move from his neck and a strange gurgling sound coming from behind.

Turning, he saw the man slumped at his feet and Blanco, with a look of horror on his face, holding a rock covered in blood.

Chapter 5

Mount Ararat

'Aaaah!'

The scream was loud and terrified. Eva whipped round to see what had caused it. She instantly wished she hadn't for she turned just in time to see one of the horses slide over the edge and down the steep scree. The horse's boy hung on to its rein for as long as he could but once it was over the edge there was little he could do but let go. The horse's hooves kicked out frantically as it tried to find a grip but it continued its inevitable journey to the bottom of the hill.

'Don't look!' said Magdalena, turning her face away.

But Eva was transfixed by the sight. The horse had reached the bottom and was still standing but was now clearly stuck down there. She glanced at the head of the column where Luca Ferron and Count Maleficio were walking. They, too, had turned at the noise and were now peering over the side. They made an incongruous couple—the Count so tall and thin and Luca Ferron so small and round. Neither of them were enjoying the journey. They were not, Eva surmised, natural travellers, both of them preferring a life of luxury and comfort and not one of perpetual motion. She was glad they were uncomfortable. It was small consolation for her captivity but it was something. She herself was sore and aching and she could only hope that they felt the same.

They had been on this pass for a few days and it was bordered on one side by a steep mountain and on the other by a sheer drop down to the river valley below. There were numerous potholes and landslides to scramble over. Eva didn't mind that, not having a fear of heights, and she took great enjoyment from watching the Count struggle to contain his fear. He was terrified of heights. It was that fear which had led to his acquaintance with Blanco, for Blanco had been the only one willing to fly the Count's experimental flying machine. The Count himself had been too scared. Some of that terror was coming back to him now as they progressed deeper into the mountains. The passes had grown increasingly narrow and difficult to cross and it was almost inevitable that something would fall. They all stared down at the stricken horse, the Count hanging well back from the edge.

'Leave it,' said Luca Ferron.

'You can't leave it!' cried Eva in horror. 'How will it get back out?'

'Do you want to go down and get it?' he asked.

Eva glared at him. She looked down at the steep scree which covered the mountainside all the way to the bottom of the valley and took a determined step forward.

'Hold her!' called Luca Ferron and Eva was grabbed by one of the many men accompanying their train. She was forced back into line and the group continued on, everyone taking even more care with their steps now. The baggage train spread out in a long untidy line behind them. The beast, which the Count had managed to fix in Constantinople, lumbered along at the end, pulled by four men.

A short time later Magdalena nearly joined the horse at the bottom of the hill. She had been trying to cross a particularly large pothole when her foot slipped and she started to slide over the edge. Only the quick actions of the man next to her saved her from sharing the same fate as the horse.

'Magdalena!' The Count came rushing to her side, concern in his face, but she waved him away.

'It's nothing,' she said. 'I'm fine.'

They continued but when they turned the next corner they were faced by a seemingly insurmountable problem. A large rock fall blocked the path and even if they could have climbed over it, there was no way the horses would be able to.

'We'll have to turn back,' Eva hissed in delight to Magdalena. She knew the longer their journey took then the more chance there was that Blanco would reach the Blue Mountain before them.

'We'll have to climb over,' said Luca.

The fear in the Count's face proved that he would never be able to manage. Even the thought of it drained his face of whatever colour it had.

'No,' he said. 'There must be another way.'

'If you won't climb it, Maleficio,' said Luca Ferron, 'then we'll leave you behind. I'll take the girl and you can take the woman and we'll meet further on.'

Magdalena and Eva gripped hands in fear.

The Count shot him a look of fury. 'No,' he said. 'We won't split up. I'll think of something.'

'Don't you trust me?' taunted Luca.

The Count glared at him.

'You'd better think quickly,' warned Luca. 'Otherwise I'm taking the rest and crossing over.'

The Count strode back down the path.

'They won't split us up, will they?' asked Eva. 'Please don't leave me with that man.'

'I think the Count's thought of something,' said Magdalena. 'Look.'

Eva turned in the direction that Magdalena was pointing. Straining against its ropes, the beast was being hauled up the slope. Eva glanced at the Count who looked delighted at another opportunity to show his experiment in action.

'God save us all,' said Magdalena, crossing herself. She and Eva had first seen the beast in action on Malta where it had almost destroyed Magdalena's convent. But Eva also knew that the firepowder that it used was highly unstable. They were lucky to have survived the explosion on the ship. Blanco had told her a lot about how it worked on Malta for he had been fascinated by it. He had also told her that the Count never got his mixtures quite right.

The baggage handlers were looking nervous. They usually had no qualms about escorting any kind of group but there was something about this one that they didn't like. Having brought the beast to the front they scarpered, muttering anxiously to themselves.

It was almost sunset before the Count deemed himself happy with the beast. He motioned for everyone to stand back.

Eva and Magdalena stood clutching hands, unsure whether they wanted it to work or not. If it didn't surely they would have to turn back. Or would Luca and the Count make them climb the rock fall? Eva couldn't imagine the Count, with his fear of heights, being able to cope.

There was an unusual silence as the Count lit the fuse. Even the mountain seemed to be holding its breath waiting to see what would happen.

It started with a quiet whoosh, the beast shuddered, and a ball of fire streaked from it straight for the rock fall. The baggage handlers stared open-mouthed, too terrified even to shout. The ball of fire slammed into the landfall and a great shower of rocks and dust flew into the air.

Even before the dust settled they could see that it had worked. A path had been cleared.

'Come on,' shouted Luca Ferron. 'Let's move!'

Wearily Eva got to her feet. She looked at her hands. Her nails were broken because of constantly gripping on to the rocks when she had to cross a path which had disappeared due to a landslide. Her feet hurt and her back ached. She could only hope that Blanco was having an easier time of it.

It was the most unusual monastery that Eva had ever seen—and she had stayed in quite a few when she and Blanco had travelled through northern Spain. It wasn't a building at all but rather a labyrinth of rooms—hundreds of them—carved into the side of a mountain. All the rooms were connected to each other—or so the monks said. Since there were thousands of them, there was no way to check. As well as the monastery there was a church and homes for all the lay-people and servants as well as wine presses, bakeries, and even some stables. The monastery was spread across thirteen separate levels—no one could be expected to find their way through it.

Perched as it was on the side of the mountain looking down two separate valleys, Magdalena thought that she had never seen a more beautiful place in her life. For the first time since the journey began she relaxed. She enjoyed being back in a daily routine that she recognized, with the bells ringing for compline or vespers bringing order to the day and night. She had spent most of her adult life in a convent after all. But she was also relieved because Luca Ferron had given the order that they would stay here and rest for a few days.

Just before they reached the monastery, Luca had pulled Eva aside. When she rejoined Magdalena her face was ashen.

'What did he say?' asked Magdalena.

Eva just shook her head and said nothing.

Luca had reminded Eva that he would kill Magdalena if she tried to escape again.

A few days later, refreshed and feeling much stronger, Magdalena decided to tackle Eva. She had noticed that Eva spent very little time in the monastery, preferring to sit outside in the sunlight rather than in the cool rooms. Eva's tension was increasing as her own lessened and she was determined to find out why.

She found Eva sitting on a ledge looking down the glorious river valley. It was green and fertile, a welcome sight after the barren mountain passes.

Eva wasn't looking at the view. She was watching Micha and Rameel flying down opposite sides of the river, studiously ignoring each other. She was so engrossed in watching them that she jumped when Magdalena sat down beside her.

'Fig?'

The monastery was surrounded by fruit trees and they had taken the chance to restock their provisions. Eva accepted the proffered fruit and bit into it. They sat in a comfortable silence for a while. From her years of experience as an abbess, Magdalena knew that the best way to get someone to talk was to stay silent.

'I'm scared,' said Eva eventually.

Magdalena turned and looked at her. Eva continued to stare fixedly down the valley, refusing to meet Magdalena's gaze.

'Of what?'

'Everything,' said Eva miserably. 'I don't like it here because I hate being in the dark. That's why I sit outside so much.'

Magdalena had forgotten Eva's fear of being underground. The caves were very similar to the underground chambers in Malta and Eva had been terrified of them.

'I'm scared that Blanco will never find us.'

Magdalena nodded.

'But most of all, I'm scared of what they're going to do to me.'

'What do you mean?'

'When we get to the mountain,' said Eva, 'the mountain where the heartstone is, I think they're going to kill me.'

Magdalena looked shocked.

'No,' she said, 'they just need you to retrieve the heartstone.'

Eva nodded glumly. 'I know, but I still think they're going to kill me. They keep calling me the sacrifice. And I have to go into the mountain. And I hate being underground. If I don't go in they might kill me.' She bit back a sob and then added quietly, 'Or you.'

Magdalena fell silent. She was furious—with herself and Marco for starting this whole thing off and with Count Maleficio and Luca Ferron for terrifying a young girl.

She hugged Eva to her. 'No they won't,' she said. 'Even if Blanco doesn't get there in time, even if the angels can't help, then I will. I won't let anyone hurt you.'

Eva wanted to believe her but she couldn't. She knew everything depended on her.

Baghdad

Baghdad rose out of the desert like a long-awaited mirage. For weeks they had seen nothing but sand and dust. Initially the golden domes of the city's mosques couldn't be seen against the sand dunes but the twists and turns of the minarets reaching up to the sky soon became apparent. It wasn't the city it once was, Gump explained to Blanco. It had been destroyed by the Mongols not long before but many of its buildings still retained their former glory. Compared to the desert, it held everything they desired.

Thankfully their camel train hadn't been threatened by any more bandit attacks. The man who Blanco had knocked out had been tied up along with any others who had been captured and kept prisoner in one of the carts.

'This is where I was looking for,' said Gump as they stopped in front of a low building.

Once inside Blanco looked around. They were in a series of rooms, all with different baths.

'It's a hamam,' said Gump. 'Public baths.'

Blanco was shocked at the idea of public bathing. He wasn't that keen on bathing in the first place, but he was filthy and had sand under his fingernails, in his hair, and ingrained in his skin.

Afterwards, he felt a lot better, the horrors of the desert felt further away and he slept properly that night for the first time in weeks.

Coming from Venice, Blanco thought that he had seen everything the merchant world had to offer but nothing could have prepared him for the wonders that were laid before him the next morning. There were enormous mounds of precious and semi-precious gemstones, piles of rubies, pearls, and emeralds. Blanco may have had no interest in following his father into the family business of precious gems but that didn't mean he was unaware of what that business involved. His sister, Angelica, would have loved all this. She had found a way of taking Blanco's place in the business—by dressing as a boy. She would have been in her element here.

Eventually Blanco found what he was looking for.

The merchant was sitting cross-legged in the middle of his shop, sipping a cup of tea. He beckoned them inside, sat them down, and poured them each some fresh mint tea. Blanco and Gump were grateful for the cooling effect, for the sun was hot. Coming from merchant families themselves they knew better than to launch immediately into sales talk. They were content to sit for a while, conversing with the merchant. Gump could remember some words of Arabic and with that, the merchant's few words of Latin, and signs they managed amicably.

After some time the merchant reached over, selected a piece of lapis lazuli from a pile beside him and handed it to Blanco. Blanco turned it over in his hands, looking at it carefully. The man then reached behind him and brought out a piece from another pile and handed that to Blanco also. They couldn't have been more different. One was highly polished and a deep indigo blue. It looked as though it had been dipped into the sky on a midwinter's night and then pulled back out with stars still clinging to it, for deep within the blue were gold sparkling lights. The other piece which Blanco held was duller, unpolished. It held the same promise of that deep blue but at the moment that promise was covered by a sheen of white chalk and small lumps of grey or white rock which still clung to it. It seemed such an innocuous stone and it was hard to believe that the heartstone would look just like it.

'Some say,' said Gump, taking the polished piece from Blanco and inspecting it for himself, 'that if you dip a piece of lapis lazuli into a pool of water you will see the entire future of the world unfold in front of you.'

'What a frightening thought,' said Blanco.

'Best quality,' said the merchant, tapping the stone in Gump's hands. It was certainly better than any that ever reached the markets of Venice.

'So this is what all the fuss is about,' said Blanco. 'A lump of stone.'

'Ah, but remember,' said Gump, 'the legend says that it is not a lump of stone, but a heart.'

'It's all nonsense though, isn't it?' asked Blanco.

Gump shrugged. He had seen more mysteries in his travels across the world than he could even remember and he wasn't one to dismiss anything. Besides, although he had exaggerated the legend, it was based on something that the people of the mountains believed in so who was he to say it wasn't true?

'Who knows?' he answered.

The merchant looked at them with interest. He hadn't seen anyone so fascinated by a piece of lapis lazuli for a long time. He was surrounded by it all day and he found it calming. It was a powerful stone, supposedly linked to divinity, and he knew that many people bought it for protection.

Blanco asked the merchant how much money he wanted. The merchant named a price and Gump surreptitiously shook his head. Blanco named a price half of the merchant's initial demand. The merchant made a face and suggested another price, slightly lower than the first, but higher than Blanco's offer. Blanco sighed.

'Keep going,' said Gump.

Blanco made another offer and the man clutched his chest dramatically as though Blanco had stabbed him in the heart but lowered his price once more.

Blanco accepted and the merchant, grinning hugely,

held out his hand for the money. Blanco handed it over and then looked again at the piece of lapis lazuli in his hand.

He knew that where they were going there would be plenty of stones like these but he had wanted to own a piece now. It would remind him of Eva and that every day he was getting closer to her. He knew without any doubt that if anything had happened, Azaz would have found him and let him know but still, he was worried. He didn't trust either Count Maleficio or Luca Ferron.

'Missing your playmate?'

Rameel materialized out of nowhere in front of Micha and she jumped with fright. She had been hovering high above the group on the ground and wondering whether she should fly on ahead to check the route or stay with Eva and Magdalena. When she and Azaz had been together he would frequently fly on and she would stay with Eva, but with him gone, she was finding it difficult to know what to do.

She was about to snap at Rameel to go away when she realized that this was a chance to talk to him. In the past she had always been with Azaz and so Rameel spent his whole time arguing and taunting for he hated Azaz with a passion. Azaz had been the leader of the rebel angels and Rameel had always been jealous of that. But he might talk to her now that she was on her own.

'What about you, Rameel?' she asked, looking at him with her beautiful golden eyes. 'Don't you get lonely flying around by yourself?'

Rameel bared his strong teeth in something that resembled a smile.

'Do you think you can get me to tell you anything just because you look at me with those big eyes?'

Micha frowned. 'I'm just trying to be friendly,' she said. 'We don't need to fight all the time. We've still got a long way to go.'

Rameel looked at her consideringly. He had always secretly admired Micha for the sacrifice she had made by choosing to fall but she had made her alliance with Azaz which meant that she couldn't be trusted.

He flew around her, too close. She stilled her own flying and dropped down slightly to get out of his way.

'Do you ever regret it?' he asked abruptly.

'What?'

'Falling.'

Micha shook her head firmly.

'Never.'

'You're lucky.'

And with that, Rameel flew away, leaving Micha staring after him in confusion. It was the first time she had ever heard him express regret.

Chapter 6

Mount Alamut

'So what saved him?' asked Blanco.

'Everyone says something different,' said Gump. 'Some say that a good physician knew the right antidote, others that someone sucked out the poison and that's how he survived.'

'I'd like to go on crusade,' said Blanco longingly.

'Why?' asked Gump. 'To fight?'

Blanco thought back to the bandit he had nearly killed during the attack on the pilgrim train and shuddered. He still had terrible nightmares about it.

'No,' he said.

'To see Jerusalem?'

Blanco shrugged, for, much as he wanted to see Jerusalem, he wasn't sure that the thought of it would be enough to make him go on crusade. 'Maybe I don't want to be a Crusader then,' he said slightly crossly. His great-uncle had a very annoying habit of making him question everything he said instead of letting him live in his dreams.

Gump had been telling him about the Assassin who had almost succeeded in killing the English king, Edward I, fifty years before, with a poisoned dagger. Edward was one of the few men to have survived an attempt on his life by the Assassins who were feared precisely because they hardly ever failed in their task. The Assassins were a group of young men who had been trained by the Old Man of the Mountain and were sent out to kill powerful enemies. They rarely attacked ordinary people and they always killed with a knife which meant that they were invariably killed themselves, especially since they never tried to escape afterwards. They lived in a beautiful castle at Mount Alamut, with stunning gardens full of fruit trees and beautiful flowers. The men who lived here thought they were living in Paradise and believed that they would return there when they had successfully completed their mission.

Now Blanco and Gump were at Mount Alamut, but it looked very different from how it had looked at the height of the Assassins' power. The castle was completely derelict and overgrown with shrubs and tree roots. Blanco found it difficult to imagine how it would have looked when it was full of people and flowers.

From where they sat Blanco and Gump could see along four river valleys, all meeting below. The castle was built on a perpendicular outcrop which hadn't been easy to climb. But presumably it had been easy to defend, which was why it had been the Assassins' headquarters.

'Are you sure you want to camp up here tonight?' asked Gump.

'Of course,' said Blanco. 'Why? Don't you think we should?'

Gump glanced over at the empty windows and doorways of the ruined castle. They were like dark howling mouths in the night. He could feel the ghosts of the Assassins hanging around the castle. It didn't feel like a safe place to camp and he felt uncomfortable.

'Maybe if we had had a chance to search the castle . . . '

'Why? Do you think someone's here?'

Now Blanco looked worried.

'No, no, I'm sure it's fine,' said Gump, rolling himself into his bed mat. He knew better than to believe in ghosts. Soon gentle snores were floating up to heaven.

After his great-uncle's words Blanco had difficulty in falling asleep. With every faint noise his eyes flew open. Noises were always so much louder and stranger in the night. He eventually gave up trying to sleep and watched as the sky grew darker and the outlines of the valley began to merge into their surroundings. The stars appeared one by one. Somewhere, hopefully not too far away, Eva was sleeping under the same stars and that thought gave him a little comfort. He started counting them, trying to work out shapes and symbols. He had never been very good at knowing which were which. He thought he could make out Orion's Belt but it could easily have been something else entirely.

As he finally drifted off the stars filled his dreams. He dreamt that he was climbing them. They were almost as difficult to climb as some of the passes they had scrambled over recently and he frequently stumbled. But they seemed quite secure and he knew that if he just kept climbing he would find Eva. She was in terrible danger but if he could reach her in time he could save her. He climbed quicker and quicker, stretching for handholds that he could barely reach.

He heard a shout and, looking up, he saw a fiery star heading straight for him. He had no choice. He rolled to one side, lost his grip, and fell.

Blanco was never sure afterwards what it was that woke him up. A shout in his ear, a rough shove, a blinding light, the sound of metal on stone, or all four. All he knew was that one moment he was fast asleep and the next he was rolling to one side as a dagger missed his head by a whisker. As he opened his eyes he was aware of two things. One was that the man trying to kill him was still hanging above him, dagger poised to strike again, and the second was that the man was in the grip of a large angel dressed in red, flowing robes.

Blanco gazed in amazement. He had never seen an angel before. This one was very tall and muscular and his flowing red robes and dark wings gave him a majestic figure. Blanco was dumbstruck and terrified.

The strange man was also terrified and Blanco realized that he had no idea how he was being held in the air.

Azaz laughed at the look on Blanco's face.

'Azaz?'

Blanco's voice emerged as a squeak.

The angel nodded and flashed him a brilliant smile. 'Good to know you can see me at last,' he said.

The stranger let out an unearthly scream which woke the sleeping Gump with a jolt.

'I knew we shouldn't have slept up here,' he said, rubbing his eyes. He seemed unperturbed by the scene which greeted him.

'Who's he?' he asked. 'And why's he standing like that?'

The Assassin did look strange, hovering in the air with his arm up, ready to strike.

'I woke up with a dagger about an inch from my nose. Azaz is holding him. And I can see him!'

'What does he look like?'

The Assassin screamed again, drowning out Blanco's reply, and then fainted.

'That's better,' said Gump getting to his feet. 'Now I can hear myself think.'

Azaz laid the Assassin on the ground and Blanco and Gump leaned over him. He stirred and they leapt back. Azaz placed a foot on his chest to stop him from rising.

Blanco crouched down.

'Who are you?' he asked.

The man glared at him in reply.

'What are we going to do with him?' asked Gump.

'I don't know,' said Blanco. 'If we let him go he might try to kill us again. Maybe we could tie him up?'

'We may as well kill him outright,' said Gump. 'If we tie him up he would starve to death up here before anyone found him.'

Gump knelt down beside the man and began to search him. He made it as difficult as possible, trying to kick out and struggle, but Blanco could see that Azaz was keeping him largely under control. Gump eventually wrestled a piece of paper from the man and read it through. Blanco peered over his shoulder but was disappointed to discover that he couldn't understand any of it. It was a very unusual style of writing.

'What does it say?' he asked.

'Hold on,' said Gump.

As he continued to read Blanco hopped from foot to foot with curiosity.

'He's the last of the Assassins,' said Gump. 'He was hired by someone to kill, and I quote, "the boy travelling with the old man. And the old man too, if possible".'

Gump said this as though someone being commissioned to kill him was an everyday occurrence.

'But who?' asked Blanco. 'Who could possibly have known that we were travelling this way?'

'The Count and the others,' he said.

'But they've gone the other way,' said Blanco. 'How could they get a message this far?'

Even as he finished the sentence the answer leapt fully formed into his head. Rameel.

'But you said an Assassin never gave up until he finished his mission,' said Blanco nervously. 'And he hasn't finished. We're still alive.'

At that moment the Assassin spoke.

'He agrees with you,' said Gump. 'He says he has to kill us.'

Blanco stared at Gump in horror.

The Assassin will have made a binding promise, interrupted Azaz. *'You have to find a way to release him from it or . . . '*

Azaz hesitated.

'Or,' prompted Blanco.

'Or you have to kill him.'

Blanco and Gump stared at each other, knowing that they were caught in a terrible dilemma. They couldn't kill the Assassin, but the moment they released him he would kill one, or even both, of them.

None of them were paying any attention to the

Assassin and so they were all taken by surprise when he threw himself at Blanco. Neither Gump nor Azaz had any time to respond. Blanco saw the knife as it glinted in the moonlight. Then the blade struck down. Blanco watched with horror as it hit his chest. He felt a heavy blow, followed by a dull pain, and the knife clattered to the ground. Almost immediately the Assassin fell on top of him, crushing him. Blanco could see Gump's dagger sticking out of his back.

'Blanco!' cried Gump, rushing over to him. 'Oh, your mother will never forgive me. This is all my fault!'

Blanco could hardly breathe. He could feel life itself being squeezed out of him. As if in a dream he watched Azaz lift the Assassin and carry him to the far side of the courtyard. With the lifting of the body, Blanco's chest filled again with air and he took a deep, spluttering breath. He began to cough and sat up.

'Blanco?'

Blanco's hands went to his chest, expecting to find blood and his life draining away. Instead, he found himself holding a piece of lapis lazuli with a large chip in it. Opening his shirt he found a big bruise and the slightest of cuts. The piece of lapis lazuli he had bought in Baghdad had just saved his life.

Chapter 7

Karakum

'Rameel! Rameel!'

Instead of answering Micha, Rameel got up and flew away, his indigo robes and wings melting into the night sky so that he became increasingly difficult to see.

Micha wasn't sure what to do. Rameel had spent the previous hour just staring at Eva. He had ignored all Micha's attempts to speak to him. Now he had disappeared.

Azaz had left Micha with two tasks. One was to watch over Eva and the other was to keep an eye on Rameel and try to find out exactly what he was planning. Micha had noticed that while Rameel had been bickering with the Count he had also been careful to avoid Luca Ferron.

Micha glanced at Eva who was lying by the fire. She was surrounded by people whose main interest was in keeping her alive until she reached Badakhshan. She would be safe for a while.

Decision made, Micha glided into the air and flew after Rameel.

Eva lay by the fire, staring fixedly into the sky, thinking of Blanco. She tried not to think about him too much for sometimes she was scared she would never see him again. She hoped he was still following her. Her mind drifted to what might happen when they reached Badakhshan. Luca had kept them to a tight schedule. He wanted to get in and out of the mountains before winter. Once winter set in the passes were impossible to cross and the area would be shut off for months. So, since the monastery in the caves they had been allowed little time to rest. They had crossed the Caspian Sea in good time and once into the desert he frequently made them march throughout the night, despite all the dangers that it held.

If there had ever been any real trust between Count Maleficio and Luca Ferron it had eroded with every passing mile. As much as Eva hated them, they hated each other even more. Tonight they were sleeping on opposite sides of the fire and Eva knew they both had knives under their pillows. The Count had insisted that Eva and Magdalena ride in front of him at all times so that he could see where they were. He was convinced that if they were out of his sight Rameel or Luca would snatch them away and leave him behind.

Eva turned her head at a sudden movement from the edge of the camp. Had Micha or Rameel come back? She stared but couldn't see an angel. Instead, through the darkness, she thought she could see the outline of a horse.

She sat up. Magdalena gave a gentle sigh and turned over. Eva was about to lie back down when she heard another noise and again caught a slight movement. Something was coming out of the shadows.

At that moment a hand was clamped over her mouth and a steely arm prevented her from struggling.

It was impossible to make any noise and when she managed to kick out her captor didn't even react. She could see that Magdalena had also been captured. Their panic-stricken eyes met briefly before they were carried away, still struggling, from the camp.

When dawn rose it found Eva and Magdalena strung over the backs of two horses, their hands and feet tied and each of them gagged with a disgusting smelly cloth. They had been travelling in this manner for most of the night. It was not, as Eva had quickly discovered, a particularly comfortable way to travel. Her blood was rushing about her ears and she felt sick. She was relieved when she felt her horse halt and she was lifted down. Although her relief only lasted until she saw the men who had captured them.

The first man was a fearsome creature. His greasy hair was tied back, he wore filthy clothes, and he had a long straggly beard. His companion, who was lifting Magdalena down from the back of his horse, was equally ugly and unkempt. When he grinned at the first man, Eva saw that most of his teeth were missing and those that remained were black.

Eva tried to glower at them but it was hard when she was so terrified. Their gags were removed and she spat, trying to rid her mouth of the horrible taste. The other man reached out a hand to touch her hair obviously unable to believe the colour of it. She turned her head and tried to bite him. He snatched his hand away and raised it to hit her but his companion shouted at him and, reluctantly, he lowered it.

'Try not to annoy them,' said Magdalena.

'Do you think they're slave traders?' muttered Eva.

Magdalena was fairly sure they were but she hid her fear from Eva.

'Whatever they are, I'm sure the others will find us soon,' she said instead.

'Not without the angels they won't,' said Eva. 'And Micha and Rameel flew off last night. I don't know when they'll come back.'

'They're waiting for something,' said Magdalena, motioning towards their captors.

'The slave train,' said Eva gloomily. She knew all about it. Groups of bandits roamed the desert, capturing where and when they could. When they had enough captives they formed them into one big slave train and they were taken to one of the cities to be sold.

The men sat down a little way from them. They were definitely waiting for something.

A little while later Eva spotted a cloud of dust on the horizon.

'That could be the Count and the others?' she said hopefully, pointing it out to Magdalena. She never thought that she would be happy to see the Count or Luca Ferron again, but, at that moment, she was.

'I think,' said Magdalena, feeling guilty for dashing Eva's hopes, 'that they're coming from the wrong direction.'

One of the men spoke but Eva could only gaze at him in incomprehension and fear. He tugged on her rope, forcing her to get up, and then did the same with Magdalena. The dust cloud grew bigger and bigger. Eventually they could make out horses and people and a long row of carts.

When the train finally ground to a halt, Eva and Magdalena were lost for words. It was much larger than they could ever have imagined and to see it materializing out of an empty desert was terrifying. There were rows of wooden carts filled with men, women, and children. There were men on horseback with whips, riding round lashing out at any arms or legs which protruded from the bars.

Two men dismounted and came over to their captors and began arguing almost straight away. At one point, one of them came over and pulled at Eva's hair, showing its colour, obviously trying to get a better price. Eva bared her teeth and the men laughed. More money was handed over. Then their captors handed the ropes which bound Eva and Magdalena to the new arrivals and they were tugged over to the train of carts.

Every captive they passed stared at them, especially at Eva's blonde hair. Eva and Magdalena were dragged to a cart with wooden bars and already full of men, women, and children.

The two friends were pushed in to join the others and then the door clanged shut behind them. Shuffling, Eva and Magdalena managed to find themselves a place against the side of the cart. Magdalena shut her eyes and started to pray. After a moment, Eva joined her, hoping that it was all a terrible dream and that when she woke up she would be back in the camp with the others.

The rough movement of the cart jolted her eyes open and she discovered that her prayer remained unanswered. They were still prisoners. Magdalena kept her eyes shut and continued to mutter prayers in Latin.

'Where are we going?' Eva asked.

A few people in the cart stared at her blankly. The others stared fixedly at the floor of the cart, lost in some world of their own. Nobody spoke. The cart trundled on.

'Rameel. We must go back. I think something has happened.'

It had taken Micha longer than she would have liked to find Rameel.

She wasn't sure that he had heard her and was about to speak again, when he said, 'Have you left Eva alone?'

Micha was puzzled by his tone. He sounded disapproving. He had been spending a lot of time hovering around Eva recently, almost protectively. She was about to answer when he spoke again.

'How do you do it?'

Micha was confused. 'What?'

'How do you manage not to interfere? How do you stop yourself from telling them what to do?'

Micha smiled a little at that. Interfering was a big problem for Azaz and she had a lot of practice in trying to stop him. She floated down until she was hovering in front of Rameel. He had his head in his arms; his voice was muffled and she couldn't see his face. If she hadn't known better, she would have thought he was crying.

'It's forbidden.'

'I know that!' snapped Rameel without looking up. 'But knowing doesn't stop us from doing it. It's a stupid rule.'

'It's not really a stupid rule,' said Micha calmly. She had had the same discussion many times with Azaz. 'If we start to interfere then we don't know how things will

change. We may think we're helping but we might be making things worse.'

'How can we make things worse? When they always get everything so wrong. The Count . . . '

'What about the Count?' asked Micha.

Rameel sighed. 'Nothing,' he said. 'The Count is just a fool.'

'What about Luca Ferron? Is he a fool too?'

Rameel stayed silent.

'You have to let go,' Micha said calmly. 'You have to let them make their own mistakes.'

'Even when they are dealing with something that's important to you?'

'What?' asked Micha. 'What are you talking about?'

'The stone.'

'The heartstone? Why are you so interested in it?'

There was silence for a moment and then Rameel raised his head. His eyes were suspiciously reddened but his face was set in sneering lines.

'I'm not,' he said. 'It's nothing to me.'

She tried again. She was sure that she hadn't imagined that note of vulnerability in his voice.

'Rameel, you know you can tell me anything.'

His face relaxed for the briefest of moments but then he laughed.

'There's nothing to tell,' he said. 'I was just seeing if you would follow me. And you did. So you failed in your duty. What will Azaz say?'

Micha glared at him.

'You're right,' he continued. 'We should go back.'

His great indigo wings unfurled and he stepped off the mountain into the air and flew off without a backward glance at her.

Feeling guilty, and with a horrible feeling that things had gone drastically wrong in her absence, Micha followed him.

Trundling through the gates of the city, Eva and Magdalena actually felt relieved, glad at least to leave the desert behind. The heat and the dust had been constant. Their throats were parched through lack of water and their lips were dry and cracked.

Eva drew Magdalena's attention to an enormous tower which seemed to soar right up to heaven. It was a glorious blue and was an amazing sight. Their cart trundled right past it and they noticed it was covered with golden carvings and inscriptions. Passing other buildings she could see that they were often covered with small blue tiles and she wondered if they were made of lapis lazuli.

The cart rolled to a stop in the centre of a large square. The men wrenched open the back of the cart and pulled the captives out one by one. Eva was dragged out so roughly she almost fell. She clung to Magdalena in fear. All around them life continued as though such behaviour happened every day, which it probably did. People shopped in the market place, merchants with their goods piled high in baskets carried on selling their wares and street cleaners swept—all seemingly unaware that in their midst was a group of people who had been snatched unwillingly in the desert and brought to be sold as slaves in this scorching town.

Eva, Magdalena, and some of the others were herded together and thrust into a dark cell, barely large enough to hold them. The only light filtered down from a hole high above them. Whenever anyone passed overhead dirt or dust fell into the cell and led to an outburst of coughing.

'They'll never find us here,' said Eva forlornly. 'The angels can't search underground.'

'Why not?'

'They're creatures of the air,' said Eva. 'Azaz told me in Malta. If they go underground they can't breathe properly.'

'That doesn't mean they won't find us,' said Magdalena firmly.

'I hope you're right,' said Eva.

It was on the fourth day of captivity that Eva heard her name called.

'Eva! Look up!'

Eva gazed up and saw Rameel. He didn't look very happy.

'I've been looking for you for days,' he said crossly, as though it was Eva's fault that she was hidden away underground. *'How did you get in here?'*

Eva scowled at him. Why did it have to be Rameel who found her, rather than Azaz or Micha.

'Can you get us out?'

Rameel shook his head.

'Not until they bring you above ground,' he said.

The cell had fallen silent when Eva spoke and quite a few of the prisoners were watching her strangely. She already stood out because of her hair colour and now they looked even more nervous about her.

'I'll come back when they bring you out,' said Rameel. 'Now that I've found you. Micha and I will find a way to rescue you.'

'What about Azaz?' asked Eva. 'Has he come back?'

Rameel shook his head again. 'No,' he said and he couldn't help looking pleased as he said it. 'We haven't seen him.'

And with that he stretched his wings and flew off, leaving Eva to explain to Magdalena what Rameel had said. Then she sat back and worried about Azaz. He shouldn't have been gone for this long. Where was he?

'I don't trust you,' said Micha flatly. 'We should wait until Azaz comes back.'

'He may be too late.'

'I'd still rather wait.'

'We can't afford to wait. Look. They're bringing them out.'

Eva and Magdalena clutched hands as they stood together in the midday heat. It was the first time they had been outside for days and they blinked in the fierce sunlight, the dust making them cough.

They stood in the market place in their bare feet. Eva looked around frantically but she couldn't see the angels. It seemed to her that the entire population of the town was staring at them. All the captives had been herded together into the middle of the square.

'Where are they?' she asked Magdalena.

'They'll come,' answered Magdalena with a calm that she didn't feel. Given that she had never seen the angels she had even more reason to doubt them than Eva.

The buyers were approaching. Eva and Magdalena stared fixedly at the ground, trying to pretend they were invisible. One man hauled Eva out of line. She was forced to let go of Magdalena's hand. He offered some money to the slave trader.

'No!' cried Eva, when she saw that the man was not interested in buying Magdalena. 'We're together!'

Both men looked at her blankly, neither of them understanding a word she said. Eva pulled Magdalena forward to show that they were together.

The buyer shook his head firmly and the slave trader pulled their hands apart. Eva kicked him and he let go and suddenly she felt herself rise up into the air. The slave traders fell to their knees in terror and bowed to the ground. She could hear the townspeople scream. She was fairly terrified herself. It reminded her of being in the flying machine with Blanco.

'Magdalena!' she screamed. 'What about Magdalena! We can't leave her!'

Magdalena was staring up at her in disbelief, ignoring the chaos that was happening around her. Everyone was screaming and running. Only Magdalena stood still, watching Eva disappear.

'We don't need her!' hissed Rameel in her ear.

'Where's Micha! Micha! Micha!'

'I left her directing the others to the meeting point. I promised her that I was strong enough to carry both of you which was the only reason she agreed.' He laughed.

'You liar!' she shrieked. 'Go back for her!'

She struggled and almost slipped from Rameel's

grasp. For an instant she was tumbling through the air. He grabbed her arms before she could fall any further.

'Be still!' he snarled. *'You're too heavy as it is!'*

They were now over the gates of the city and Eva couldn't see the market square or hear the shrieks of the people any more. She could see the minaret and knew that Magdalena was standing under it. But unless she wanted to fall—and what good would that do Magdalena?—she had to stop struggling and let Rameel take her back. She would send Micha back for Magdalena.

They flew for a long time. Eva began to ache and she longed to be put down but her pride stopped her from asking. Eventually Rameel began to fly lower and Eva recognized their long baggage train with the lumbering beast at the end. When Rameel dropped her, she fell to her knees and started to cry. It had been bad enough travelling with Magdalena. How was she going to manage without her?

She was sobbing when she felt a hand on her shoulder. Looking up, expecting the Count or Luca Ferron, she was amazed when she saw Magdalena. She threw her arms around her in delight and disbelief.

'I thought Rameel had left you!'

Magdalena disentangled herself from Eva's embrace. *'I brought her.'*

Eva turned at the beloved voice and saw Azaz.

'You've come back!' she cried joyfully. 'Tell me about Blanco. Tell me everything.'

Chapter 8

Herat

Blanco had never seen anything as beautiful as the gardens of Herat. After the dryness and monotony of the desert he couldn't believe the lushness of the valley they found themselves in. There were deep purple, brilliant blue, scarlet red, and bright orange flowers everywhere they looked as well as trees heavily laden with fruit. It had been a long hard journey since their adventure at Mount Alamut. Over the weeks they had crossed rivers, traversed valleys, climbed high mountains and trudged for days along rubble-strewn deserts. There were many times when Blanco was sure they would never reach Badakhshan. They had to travel through the baking sun of the day which scorched their skin and the icy cold of the nights which froze their bodies to the core. They had met many people on their way, some friendlier than others, but none since the Assassin had tried to kill them. They had often stopped at small villages where they had been invited to share the yurts and food of the travelling herders. While tasty, the food had grown monotonous over the weeks so it was with delight that the first thing Blanco saw once they were within the walls of Herat was a tree laden with peaches. Reaching up he picked one and bit into it. It was delicious and he quickly devoured it, even catching the juice as it tried to escape down his chin.

Herat was a strange mix of destruction and beauty. There were many buildings which, Gump told him, had been destroyed almost a century before by Genghis Khan, a fighter who had swept across this whole area, destroying everything in his path. There were also many new buildings which were ornately decorated with tiles and mosaics in shades of turquoise, aquamarine, and sunshine. Taken all together the city felt fresh and cool and Blanco found it extremely welcoming after the harshness of their journey so far. Although it was imperative that they reach the mines before Eva and the others he thought that they could afford to have a few days' rest here. They were so close after all and Gump said they had made good time.

He looked in awe at a high wooden door decorated with small blue tiles. Lapis tiles.

'There's so much of it around,' said Blanco. 'Why is this one stone so important when you can find it everywhere.'

'Because legend says it isn't a stone,' said Gump. 'It's a heart.'

Throughout the journey Blanco and Gump had talked about many things but they had studiously avoided talking about the stone and the powers it may possess. Before they set off, Gump had maintained that it was nothing, just a stone, and that the 'legend' was only a story that had gained importance over time.

Blanco had always been a little more sceptical. He couldn't believe that the Count and Luca Ferron would go to so much trouble over something that had no power. This was the first time he had heard Gump say that he thought it could be anything more than just a stone. As he was about to ask him more Gump stopped his horse and knocked on a door.

'I had a friend who lived here,' he said.

'And you think he'll still be . . . here?' Blanco had been about to say 'alive' since his great-uncle was the oldest man he knew but he thought it would be rude.

Gump's eyes twinkled as he realized what Blanco meant but before he could reply the door opened and a young man stood there. Gump spoke and they were waved inside.

Blanco looked around. He was in a large room, sparsely but exquisitely furnished. The door swung open and a whole line of people, each bearing a tray of food, came in. Blanco's eyes lit up at the sight. The first tray was heaped with rice mixed with nuts, fruits, and meats. The next contained chicken cooked in a colourful sauce and the third was filled with lamb. There were also aubergines and meatballs. The smell from the trays was tantalizing and Blanco couldn't keep his stomach from rumbling.

A laugh came from the doorway. The old man standing there waved at the food which now sat upon a low table in front of Blanco.

'Please,' he said. 'Eat.'

Blanco didn't need a second invitation.

★ ★ ★

'There is one place you must go before heading for the Blue Mountain. You must go to the prophet at the Minaret of Jam.'

They were sitting cross-legged on cushions on the floor. Gump was explaining to his old friend why they had travelled so far. Mufti had remained silent through Gump's tale but as soon as Gump stopped he mentioned the prophet.

'Why do we need a prophet?' asked Blanco. 'We know where we're going—and we know what we're going to find when we get there.'

'The young are always so impatient,' sighed Gump.

'They think they know everything,' agreed Mufti. He turned to Blanco. 'It won't take you far out of your way but I really think you should speak to him. He is a very wise man. You are strangers in the area—he might tell you something helpful.'

'I do have friends in the mountains,' said Gump. Then he frowned. 'At least I had forty years ago.'

'Still,' said Mufti, 'it is a dangerous place. You should accept all the help that you can.'

If Blanco thought their journey had been difficult before then he was mistaken, for this was where it really got difficult. They were frequently left struggling for breath as they climbed the mountains. For a start, there was less air for them to breathe. The higher they climbed the more difficult it became to scramble over the rocks. The map that Mufti had given them led them deeper and deeper into the mountains and Blanco could feel them closing in around him. They towered over him, dwarfing him, making him feel small and, sometimes, scared.

'Are you sure this is the right way?' he asked.

'That's the fourth time you've asked me today,' Gump snapped. 'Do you want to read the map?'

'No, no, I trust you,' said Blanco. 'It's just everything looks the same.'

They were trying to find the Minaret of Jam where the prophet lived. Mufti had been so insistent that Blanco had been persuaded that it would be worth the small detour.

They were deep within a mountain pass. Every so often, when their way was blocked, they crossed the river and walked on the other side for a while. Then, when that side was blocked they crossed over again. Sometimes it was easy. They just jumped or waded across the icy water. At other times, the water was deeper and they had to throw rocks in to help them get a secure footing or lift branches which stretched over. The sheer walls of the mountains reached up forbiddingly, denying them access upwards. Their only choice was to follow the river and hope for a break in the ridge. Sometimes it seemed as though it would never come.

'Do we have to go over any of these?'

Blanco eyed the towering peaks with trepidation. At the moment, he couldn't imagine anything worse. He was relieved, therefore, when his great-uncle shook his head.

'No,' he said. 'We're on the Hari Rud river now. It should lead us straight to the minaret.'

Blanco was happy about that—what could be easier than following a river?

The answer lay around the next bend. The track turned into a sheer precipice which disappeared into a fast-flowing torrent of water. A torrent that was too fast for them to cross on foot. Even if they could have done so, the other side was just as sheer. The only way to go was up.

Now Blanco knew why he had fingers. They were useful for a lot of things, of course, but they were absolutely indispensable when it came to clinging to the side of a rock face and trying to manoeuvre sideways. Sometimes, as he scrabbled for a toe- or foothold they were the only things stopping him from falling into the raging river below. He didn't dare look down. He didn't want to see how far he would drop. Instead he stared at the beige-coloured rocks in front of him and reached sideways one more time.

'Put your feet and hands where mine were,' said Gump.

He sounded calm and sure and that gave Blanco some comfort. If a man of Gump's age could manage then so could he. He tried to watch where Gump was placing his hands and feet but it wasn't always easy to see. He reached for a rock and was about to swing his weight over when it suddenly crumbled in his hand. The pieces tumbled down like a collection of bouncing balls. He clutched at thin air for a moment and tried to keep his balance as his left hand grasped for something, anything, to hold on to. He dislodged about three handfuls of earth before his hand found a rock that didn't move. He grabbed it firmly and hung like a star with his two feet and two hands splayed as wide as they could be. He was too terrified to move. How, he wondered, could he fly a machine from a great height and yet be scared of climbing?

'There's a path here!' shouted Gump in the distance. Blanco couldn't tell how far ahead he was for he was too scared to turn his head to look.

'Great,' he muttered into the stone his head was pressed up against.

'Come on! Why aren't you moving?'

Blanco forced himself to turn his head but even that action caused a small landslide and he froze, sure that he was about to fall.

Gump's voice, when it came again, sounded a little closer.

'Just take your right hand and place it on the spur above your head.'

Blanco couldn't.

'Blanco, you have to. Otherwise you'll never be able to move. Do you want to be here when night falls?'

The thought of still clinging to the mountainside in the darkness terrified Blanco.

Trembling, he lifted his hand from its current spot and transferred it to the rock above his head.

'Now take your right foot . . . '

Limb by limb, spur by spur, rock by rock, Gump talked Blanco across the landslide until he was standing safely on the path on the other side. There his legs gave out and he collapsed on the ground.

'Just for a moment,' he gasped. 'I need to get my breath back.'

Gump patted him on the back. 'Well done.'

★ ★ ★

They almost missed the minaret for it blended in so well with its surroundings. Once they were close enough they found it striking. There had been minarets in Herat and in Baghdad and many of the other places they had been, but none compared to this one. It stretched high into the sky like a finger pointing straight at heaven and was the only man-made structure in the area. It was strange to see it surrounded by mountains but it seemed to fit in. It was in three sections, with each section getting narrower as it approached the top. There was writing etched into the bottom part and Gump reached out a hand and traced some of the letters.

'What does it say?' asked Blanco.

'I don't know,' said Gump. 'I don't recognize the language.'

Leaning back he looked upwards. About two thirds of the way up the first section, before it reached a balcony, there was a layer of blue tiles. Apart from that it stood, the same colour as the hillsides, blending in with them, a man-made tower trying to equal the height of the mountains which surrounded it.

'Hello!'

Blanco shouted but even though his cry echoed right across the valley, no reply came.

'I don't think anyone's here,' he said. 'Shall we go up?'

Gump shook his head. 'I'm exhausted,' he said. 'I'll stay down here. You go.'

Blanco stepped inside, glad of the coolness of the interior: the sun was merciless and they had been walking all day. He was surprised to be greeted by two staircases, one on each side. He guessed it didn't matter which side he chose. They both led to the top.

By the time he got to the balcony at the end of the first section he was severely out of breath. That didn't stop him from leaning out and calling down to his great-uncle. Gump was lying in the sunshine, his feet dipped in a small stream, trying to get cool. Lazily, he waved up at Blanco.

Blanco caught his breath as he looked at the amazing view spread out in front of him. It was spectacular at this level so he couldn't wait to see what it was like from the top. Wave after wave of mountains broke before him and he could see the full length of the valley, the river turning and twisting like a length of silver ribbon.

He continued climbing. A dappled light filtered in from cunningly disguised windows so he could see where he was going. He could barely breathe by the time he climbed the last step and emerged onto the platform at the top. When he lifted his head what little breath he had left was snatched away.

There was an old man sitting against the far wall.

The man gave no sign that he had noticed Blanco's noisy eruption onto the platform. His eyes were closed and there was a faint humming sound coming from between his lips. He had long white hair and wore a white robe and radiated stillness.

Having regained both his breath and his balance Blanco took a hesitant step forward.

'Hello?' he said quietly.

The old man's eyes opened and Blanco stared into pools of intense blue. They were the same colour as the piece of lapis that he still carried. The man waved for Blanco to come closer. More than a little scared, Blanco obeyed.

'I have something to tell you,' said the man in flawless Latin. 'You must ask nothing. Only listen. Sit.'

Blanco sat, staring open-mouthed at the white-robed figure.

'You have come on a long journey.'

He paused. Blanco nodded.

'You are seeking a great treasure which lies in the Blue Mountain.'

Again Blanco nodded.

'The Blue Mountain is a jealous mountain. If you take something from her then she will require a sacrifice in return.'

Blanco frowned at this. The Count's diary, which Blanco had read in Malta, frequently referred to Eva as the sacrifice. He wanted to ask the man if Eva had to be the sacrifice but he was too scared to speak.

'That sacrifice will be made out of love.'

Blanco frowned. Eva wouldn't go into the mountain for love. She wouldn't go in unless she was made to. She hated being underground. And she certainly didn't love Count Maleficio or Luca Ferron.

'What is taken will be returned to the one who buried it.'

'But . . . ' interrupted Blanco, 'no one knows . . . '

The old man was still speaking. 'One will have to stay behind to take its place.'

The old man's eyelids closed back over his deep blue eyes. Blanco was confused. If the stone was to be returned to the one who put it there then Eva must come back out with it. But if someone had to stay behind then did that mean she wouldn't come back out? Did that mean that someone would go in with her? Might that be him? His own heart leapt with fright at the thought. Much as he wanted to protect Eva, he wasn't convinced that he wanted to be buried alive.

'What do you mean? Who put it there?'

The old man kept his eyes closed and said nothing.

Blanco rose to his feet. It had been an angel who had put the stone there—and that had been thousands of years ago. How could they find him? He decided to go back down since the old man was clearly not going to answer any questions. He had taken two steps when he heard the voice again.

'Not all will return.'

Chapter 9

Badakhshan

'Could you imagine how quick it would be if we could just fly over these mountains?' said Blanco, dreaming aloud. It was his love of flying machines that had led him to Count Maleficio in the first place and he still dreamed of ways of flying. 'No bandits, no need to find water, no scrambling over passes.'

'No chance of it happening either,' retorted Gump. 'Never heard anything so stupid in my life. Flying over mountains indeed.'

Blanco sighed. His great-uncle, adventurous in so many ways, just couldn't imagine getting anywhere by flying. It made perfect sense to him. It would save all this walking. Since leaving the Minaret of Jam, their way hadn't got any easier. The mountains were just as high, the passes just as difficult. But Blanco was beginning to enjoy the beauty of them. He loved being surrounded by the high peaks, walking with the river gushing in the valley below. He loved being encased in a dark valley and then turning a corner to find another wave of mountains stretching out ahead, another valley to walk through. He loved falling asleep outside and waking periodically through the night to see how far the moon and the stars had travelled in their own journey across the night sky.

'Pull me up!'

Gump looked down from his vantage point at the top of the pass. Blanco was struggling up the last few yards. He was now much better at negotiating the steep mountain passes but he would never be a natural climber. Gump reached down and pulled him over the last step.

'There it is,' he said, pointing down the valley. 'The Blue Mountain.'

Blanco stared at it. It towered over the others, hanging over the valley like a dark cloud. It didn't look very welcoming.

Since leaving the Minaret of Jam they had walked solidly, making good time. They had crossed some scary passes and Blanco had thought that he would fall more than once. He could never get used to the fact that he could be walking along a path quite confidently and it would just suddenly disappear. Then he would have to scramble over a load of rubble. This was never easy as the rubble frequently started slipping down the mountainside.

A dog barked suddenly and Blanco reached down and picked up a stone. They had come across a lot of wild dogs in these parts and some of them were prone to attack for no reason. They continued along the path, round a corner and found a child in the middle of the track. Another child came running up and together they stared at the two strangers.

The villages here were built into the mountain

which meant that they were rarely spotted until Blanco and Gump were practically on top of them. Barking dogs and small children were the first sign that a seemingly uninhabited valley was, in fact, full of people. Although sometimes greeted with suspicion they had also found many warm welcomes and were usually given something to eat and somewhere to sleep. Having spent the first couple of occasions sleeping inside the house, Blanco soon learnt to copy his great-uncle and join him on the roof. There, the cool night breeze kept away the smells from the fire and any biting insects. The houses lacked windows and soon grew stuffy. Sleeping on the roof was definitely preferable.

A man appeared behind the two children and stared at them with curiosity. Then, he waved towards his house.

'Chai?' he said.

Once replete with chai and bread they continued on towards the Blue Mountain. Gump looked at Blanco as they walked. Over the months they had been travelling Blanco had grown taller and also broadened out. He no longer looked like the young boy who had set off to build a flying machine over a year ago. His hair was long and straggled round his shoulders. Gump had offered to cut it but Blanco had decided not to let his great-uncle loose on it with a blunt knife. He had picked up different items of clothing on the way—either swapping his own with other travellers or discarding them in favour of local clothes. He was now wearing a long loose tunic which had once been white and was now the colour of dust, baggy leggings of a slightly darker hue and a belt slung loosely round his waist. On his head was a dark brown woollen hat with a rim, given to him by one of the villagers they had stayed with after Herat. Blanco had swapped it for his Venetian cap. Gump was proud of him and gave him a hefty pat on the back. Blanco wasn't expecting it and stumbled forward.

'What was that for?' he asked in surprise.

'Nothing,' said Gump. 'Come on, let's keep moving. I want to reach the village before nightfall.'

They were stopped long before they reached the mountain. The trade in lapis lazuli was a lucrative one and there were scouts scattered throughout the region watching out for any thieves. Blanco and Gump were spotted as soon as they entered the valley.

They were knee-high in a freezing glacial river when six men rose up in front of them. Casting a quick look around Blanco saw that there were another four behind.

'What do we do now?' he asked Gump.

The men were shouting at them, one in particular seeming to take the lead.

'What are they saying?' asked Blanco.

Gump frowned.

'They're telling us to turn back.'

Blanco gaped at him in horror. How could they turn back now? They were so close.

'Tell them we can't,' he suggested.

Gump shouted across the river.

A sharpened stick just missed Blanco and splashed in the river beside them.

'I don't think they want to negotiate,' said Gump.

As Blanco and Gump stared at each other in indecision the men surrounding them all brought out sticks, spears, or knives.

Blanco and Gump began to edge backwards, aware that the men behind them were just as heavily armed. The man who had been shouting the most raised his arm and the next moment a rain of sticks fell on and around them.

'Ouch!' cried Blanco as one struck his leg. It hadn't gone in too deeply but even so, when he pulled it out blood trickled down his leg. The leader of the men laughed. He seemed to be enjoying taunting them.

He shouted again.

'What did he say?' asked Blanco.

Gump had gone pale. 'Kill them,' he said.

The men were splashing through the water towards them and there was nowhere for Blanco or Gump to turn. They each pulled out a knife determined to at least go down fighting.

A loud horn sounded across the river. It could be heard even above the splashing and shouting and the men stopped. Peering past them Blanco could see another group of men on the far river bank. The old man standing there shouted something and reluctantly the men parted. Only one man refused, the one who had ordered them to be killed. He was clearly having an argument with the old man. The old man listened for a while and then dismissed him with a disparaging wave of his hand. The younger man flushed bright red and looked furious. He glared at Blanco and Gump.

The old man waved for Blanco and Gump to come forward. When they were almost at the bank he smiled a wide toothless grin.

'Marco!' he cried with delight.

Gump frowned and then his brow cleared. 'Saifullah!' he called. In moments the two old men had embraced.

'This is my great-nephew, Blanco,' said Gump, motioning Blanco forward. Blanco found his hand being grasped and kissed.

'And this is my son, Faisal,' said Saifullah.

Blanco and Gump turned and saw the man who had ordered them killed only moments before. He scowled and stormed off.

Still not entirely sure how he got there, Blanco found himself sitting beside a fire, with a bowl of chai in his hands. His great-uncle sat on the far side, chatting animatedly to the man who had embraced him earlier. Occasionally he would look over and wink at Blanco. Blanco could only assume that Saifullah was an old friend of his great-uncle's.

He looked round the village. Like many of the others, it was built into the mountainside. The light from the fire showed how the houses were all stacked on top of each other. They used both the mountain and the roofs and walls of the other houses to build on to. The light from the fire also threw up the faces of the others seated round it. Most appeared friendly enough. They made no attempt to talk to Blanco but they would occasionally nod at him and offer him some of the leaves they were chewing. Blanco had accepted the first time but the taste was so strong and unpleasant that he had spat it out into his hand (although he made sure no one saw him) and had refused all offers since.

Gump and his friend talked for a long time. The villagers drifted off one by one until there was only Gump, Saifullah, and Blanco left. Blanco was just about to ask where he could sleep when Gump turned to him.

'Saifullah wants to tell you about lapis lazuli.'

Saifullah nodded his wizened old head and grinned over at Blanco before starting to speak.

'First of all,' said Gump, translating for Saifullah, 'you have to understand that lapis is a part of our lives. My father and his father and his father before him and all the way back for as long as anyone can remember mined for lapis lazuli in these mountains. It has been so for hundreds of years. We placate the mountain before we take her precious jewels from her and that is why she allows us to take her treasure. Over the years we have learned the best ways to do this and she has rained blessings down on us. But the rituals are important and those who take from her without asking do so at their peril.'

Blanco wanted to ask what the rituals were but Saifullah was still talking.

'The mountain yields three jewels to us. First, and most frequently, a pale blue stone which we call asmani. It is the colour of the sky on a summer's day, the white embedded in it is like clouds. A rarer stone, sabzi, is blue like the river with channels of green, like the plants which grow underwater, running through it. But rarest of all are the bloodstones, the nili. They are a dark indigo blue, with red undertones. They look like the night sky with gold stars trapped within. We say the nili are a map of the world. They are very powerful.'

'Which is this one?' asked Blanco. He pulled out the stone that he had bought months ago in Baghdad.

Saifullah leaned over and took the stone from Blanco's hand. He considered it in the reflection of the firelight.

'This is a good stone,' he said, turning it round and round so that the gold stars shone. 'It is one of the bloodstones. From our second mine. I can show you the seam it came from.'

'You can tell which mine each stone is from?' asked Blanco admiringly.

'Of course,' replied Saifullah. 'These stones are my life. I know every one of them. I imagine some of them on their great journeys, travelling to places that I will never see, but delighting in the fact that the jewels from my mountain are carried across the world. They are my eyes.'

'Have you ever left here?'

The old man shook his head when Gump put the question to him. 'Why would I? The whole world is here. Why seek out other places? You can search forever but what you want is always in your own heart and not in a faraway land.'

Blanco fell silent for a moment.

'What about the heartstone?'

Gump asked Saifullah. Saifullah listened and then laughed. Then spoke for some time. Gump frowned.

'What is it?' asked Blanco.

Gump waved him to silence and carried on listening. Eventually he turned to Blanco.

'He says there is no heartstone. He says it's just a legend.'

Having finally wrapped himself snugly in his blankets, Blanco turned to his great-uncle for some answers.

'Why does Saifullah's son keep scowling at us?' he asked.

'Faisal was a horrible little boy,' said Gump, 'and it seems he hasn't improved. I'd keep out of his way if I were you.'

Blanco had already decided to do exactly that.

'Why is he so angry?'

'Faisal thinks that Saifullah is too old and that he should abdicate the leadership to him. By not letting him kill us, Saifullah has embarrassed him in front of the villagers. He's persuaded most of the young men in the village that he should be leader but the older men still want Saifullah,' continued Gump. 'If the younger men win they'll soon learn their mistake. Saifullah is a wise and thoughtful leader. Faisal will be cruel and vindictive.'

Blanco said nothing. The argument between Faisal and his father reminded him of his own family. His sister hated Blanco because it was his right, as the son, to inherit the family business even though he didn't want it and she did.

'The others can't be here yet.'

'No. Saifullah says there's been no sign of them. They get very few visitors up here and as you now know, strangers are noticed immediately. The lapis trade is a rich one. They have to protect it.'

'So, we did get here first.'

'I told you we would,' said Gump.

'And what about the heartstone?'

'The one that Saifullah says doesn't exist?' Gump laughed. 'The old fox. He used to play practical jokes on me all the time when I was here last. His father was the one who told me the legend. And now he tells me it's not true!'

'Maybe it isn't. Maybe we really have come all this way for nothing.'

'Whether we have or not one thing's certain. The Count's plan won't work. They don't let women on the mountain, so Eva won't be allowed to go.'

'Why not?'

As Blanco asked the question he realized that there had been no women in the village.

'Because the mountain is a female and gets jealous if another female sets foot on it. The villagers aren't prepared to risk it. Even their families live further down the valley.'

Blanco fell silent at that. Would that be enough to stop the Count and Luca? He lay on his back looking up at the stars which seemed even bigger and brighter here. The silhouettes of the mountains were like big jagged teeth against the dark blue sky. Somewhere out there, just beyond these mountains, was Eva. And she was coming closer every day.

Neither of them was aware of the dark angel hovering overhead, listening to every word they said. He looked at them as they lay there and then sank down next to them. He would spend the night here. He didn't want to miss a thing.

Chapter 10

The sun woke Blanco early the next day as it peered over the mountains. He had placed his blankets the night before so that when he woke in the morning he would be staring straight at the Blue Mountain. The dawn light hadn't reached it yet and it was still cloaked in darkness. Blanco wondered what secrets lay hidden beneath its surface. The sun's rays caressed the highest peaks first and then slowly spread their embrace across the lower peaks. As he watched, the shadows on the Blue Mountain began to scatter and he could distinguish different features and colours. The snow on the highest peaks was a strong pure white. It had never been walked on.

Something caught his eye and he turned his head. For a moment Blanco thought he saw an angel in dark blue robes curled up, head tucked under his wings, fast asleep. But when he looked again there was nothing. He rubbed his eyes vigorously. He must have been imagining things.

He stretched, yawning loudly, and woke his great-uncle.

'It's impossible to get a decent night's sleep with you around,' grumbled Gump. 'If it's not assassins or wild animals then it's loud noises and sunshine.'

Blanco laughed. He was feeling much better about

everything and filled with a new confidence. They were here. They had beaten the others. He was going to save Eva and then they were going to go home. But there was something he wanted to do first.

'Gump,' he said, turning to his great-uncle who was trying to get back to sleep, 'do you think they'll let me go into the mines to see how they work?'

Blanco regretted his request long before he reached the mines. Throughout their journey they had been forced to climb some steep mountain passes but nothing compared to this. The route was practically vertical. Blanco was struggling for breath almost immediately and he dared not look down. He wasn't helped by the fact that Faisal was right behind him and kept catching his feet. Whenever Blanco glared at him, Faisal just waved a hand upwards as though telling him to hurry up. Blanco gritted his teeth and followed closely in Saifullah's footsteps. The few times he had stepped out on his own he had started a small landslide. He quickly learnt to place his feet directly into the marks left by Saifullah.

Blanco forced himself to ignore the ache in his legs and kept putting one foot in front of the other. His only view was of Saifullah's bare soles. He tried looking down a couple of times, but even if he could ignore Faisal's scowling face, he didn't like it. He felt dizzy and the thought of tumbling back down the slope terrified him.

Blanco was concentrating so hard that when Saifullah finally came to a stop, Blanco crashed into him. Saifullah laughed and grabbed hold of Blanco before he could fall. He said something but Blanco could only shake his head in frustration because he couldn't understand him. His great-uncle had found the language came back to him—he had spent nine months alone here after all—but Blanco couldn't understand a word. As so often on his journey he had to rely on a form of sign language. He wished his great-uncle were here but Gump had stayed down in the village, saying he had climbed enough mountains for the time being.

They had stopped at a large cave which seemed to disappear into the mountain. Lying outside it were piles of whitish rock, some with glints of blue in them, some without. The cave-mouth was completely black and covered with what Blanco soon worked out was soot.

Saifullah pointed out some of the entrances to the other mines. Blanco made a sign like a heart and then pointed at the mine entrances but Saifullah just laughed and clapped him hard on the back. Blanco guessed that that meant that Saifullah had no intention of telling him in which mine the heartstone lay. Instead he motioned Blanco towards the nearest entrance. Blanco hesitated only momentarily. He had spent a lot of time underground in the chambers in Malta but there was still something a little strange about walking into the side of a mountain. From the way that Saifullah had spoken about them last night they were living things. Taking a last breath of clean fresh mountain air, Blanco stepped forward. He was soon enveloped in darkness and had to give his eyes time to adjust before he could move on.

As he walked further in the heat became overpowering. The sun had been hot. But that was nothing compared to the heat inside the mountain. The walls closed in around him and all he could see was a flickering torch in front of him. Soon he had to duck down as the roof got lower and lower. At the same time the noise of tapping got louder and louder. All along the passageway the walls and roof were streaked black with soot. Blanco couldn't imagine Eva in such a place. She had been terrified in the Maltese chambers and they had been much higher and wider than these tunnels.

Blanco could see Saifullah in front of him by the light of the torch he was carrying and he could sense Faisal behind him: Faisal was dogging his footsteps so closely that he was virtually breathing down his neck. When they came to a stop Faisal bumped hard into Blanco and Blanco knew he had done it deliberately. He didn't understand why Faisal hated him so much.

They had stopped at the point where the lapis lazuli was being extracted. Four men were taking it in turns to strike the rock face. When large lumps fell off the men would pick them up and throw them into a pile. Blanco guessed that most of them would be taken outside for inspection. The light wasn't strong enough in here for them to check the quality.

He watched in confusion as they lit a fire. The smoke billowed out from it, taking away whatever fresh air there was left. Blanco coughed and spluttered but the men seemed used to it. After the fire had been burning against the rock face for a while, the men doused it and then threw water on to the burnt area and began to strike again. The fire made the rock splinter more easily.

Saifullah motioned for one of the men to give

Blanco a hammer. The man gladly did so. It was heavier than Blanco had expected but he was determined not to look stupid or weak in front of Faisal. He swung the hammer as he had seen the other men do. It cracked hard against the rock and Blanco bounced back with the force of the blow. Faisal let out a scornful laugh but his father glared at him and he stopped. Once recovered, Blanco waited to see if any piece would fall off but the rock face remained stubbornly solid.

Saifullah motioned at the hammer, indicating that Blanco should try again. First, though, he asked one of the miners to show Blanco the best way to strike. Apparently it was better to hit at an overhang than directly at the rock face, and preferably at the bits which were most covered with soot.

The heat was sapping Blanco's energy but he lifted the hammer and struck again at the rock. He shut his eyes as he did so, in anticipation of the pain which would shoot up his arms. But this time there was none, only a large crack and then a cheer from the men. He opened his eyes and found a small piece of rock at his feet. Grinning, Saifullah picked it up and presented him with it. Blanco happily accepted. His own piece of lapis lazuli mined by his own hands. He knew what he was going to do with it. He was going to give it to Eva.

In the mountains

'They don't trust each other,' said Magdalena indicating the Count and Luca Ferron. 'They may have been partners once but it was an unholy alliance. They only banded together because they had to and now that they are getting closer to their prize, each of them wants it for himself.'

'I thought they were going to share it?' said Eva.

'Each is scared the other is going to run off with it. And one of them will. They were never going to share it.'

Eva said nothing but she was thinking that if she was the one who had to go in to get the heartstone, then maybe she would keep it for herself.

They had stopped on their upward trek as the two men argued. Their baggage handlers straggled along the path behind them, carrying all the belongings, including the Count's alchemical equipment which had been brought all the way from Venice. Eva and Magdalena were perched on a rock looking back at the steep mountain pass they had just climbed over.

'At least it makes a change from the desert,' said Eva.

'Well, that's true,' admitted Magdalena, although it was a scant blessing. She came from a country without hills never mind monstrous mountains like these and she was finding the passes extremely difficult.

'It's beautiful here,' said Eva, looking at the mountains which encircled them. 'I don't think I've ever seen anywhere so beautiful in all my life.'

Magdalena looked at her in surprise. Eva had become increasingly strained during the last few weeks in the desert, particularly as the fighting had increased between the Count and Luca. It had served to make Eva increasingly aware of the danger she would be in when they reached their destination. Yet now that they were closer, she was more relaxed.

Eva saw the confusion on Magdalena's face. 'I know,' she said. 'It doesn't make sense. But I feel at home in these mountains. And there's something else.'

'What?'

'I just know that Blanco is near,' she smiled.

'He's here,' said Rameel. 'Behind those rocks up there.'

'Is he alone?' asked the Count.

'No,' said Rameel, 'he has some friends with him. I think they plan to attack you.'

'Oh really,' said Luca, the smile back on his face at those words. 'I think not. Maleficio, shall we give them a demonstration?'

The Count and Luca Ferron might have been arguing only moments before but they seemed in complete accord over this. They motioned one of the bearers forward. Eva came with him.

'Who is it?' asked Eva, coming forward. A sudden thought crossed her mind. 'Is it Blanco?'

Rameel shook his head. 'Wait and see,' was all he said.

Faisal and his friends had hidden themselves in the mountains above the path.

A few days earlier, not long after Blanco had gone into the mines, Faisal had heard from one of the scouts that another group of strangers had entered the valley. Faisal was determined that this group would not reach the Blue Mountain. Blanco and Gump might be under the protection of his father but this new group wasn't and if he wanted to kill them, then kill them he would.

Faisal counted the number of people in the party.

There were four at the head. Behind them were men from further down the valley who were pulling on heavily loaded donkeys and looking about anxiously. They knew the dangers that lay in wait for them in these mountains. Faisal was notorious throughout the valleys for not letting strangers near the Blue Mountain and he guessed that they must have been paid well to take the risk. But had they been paid well enough to lose their lives?

The group had stopped. The two men in the lead were looking straight at Faisal's hiding place. But they couldn't know they were there, could they?

The men motioned to the bearers to bring forward one of the donkeys and the tall thin one removed something from one of the panniers. Faisal couldn't work out what it was. He couldn't decide whether to attack or not. He had a feeling that he had lost the element of surprise. He was about to crawl away, further out of sight, and come up with a new plan when, suddenly,

BOOM!

The noise reverberated round the valley causing the ground under their feet to shake as it sometimes did when the mountain got angry. Faisal's companions howled with fear and ran off but Faisal stayed where he was. The thing, whatever it was, had definitely been aimed at them. Terrified by what kind of demon could cause such a noise, but determined not to show fear, he rose to his feet and held up his hands.

Luca Ferron and Count Maleficio had learned from Rameel all about Faisal, the disgruntled son of the village leader. Now they had a use for him. They motioned him down and, slowly, Faisal obeyed.

Chapter 11

It was over a week since they had arrived and Blanco couldn't help noticing that Faisal was no longer scowling at him all the time. That morning Faisal had almost smiled at him.

'Something's up,' he said to Gump.

'There's always something up with you,' said Gump, although he smiled affectionately as he said it.

Staying in one place for a while had given them a chance to regain their strength. All Blanco had been doing for days was eating and sleeping. But he had also noticed that every day Faisal had walked about encased in a thick cloud of bitterness and the scowl had never moved from his face. But today he was smiling, smirking almost, and Blanco was suspicious. He just wished he knew why.

'It's Faisal,' said Blanco. 'He's looking too happy.'

'You've been moaning all week that he keeps scowling at you.'

'I know,' said Blanco, 'that's why I think something's up.'

He stared at Faisal. Faisal, feeling his look, scowled back and kicked a stone in his direction. Blanco suddenly felt much better.

'What are we going to do?'

'About Faisal?'

'No,' said Blanco, 'about the heartstone. And Eva. And everything. It's all very well sitting here in the village but what are we going to do?'

'We're going to save them.'

'How?'

'I don't know.'

Blanco looked at his great-uncle with some exasperation. Blanco had been determined to follow Eva, and Gump had gone along with it, but they had never actually worked out what they were going to do once they reached Badakhshan. And now, here they were, and they still didn't know.

'Maybe we could try to find the heartstone ourselves.'

Gump laughed and waved a hand, taking in the mountains surrounding them.

'Where would you like to start?'

Blanco scowled. 'We've got to do something.'

Gump nodded. 'We will,' he said, 'we will. We'll talk about it tomorrow.'

Blanco wasn't sure what woke him. It could have been a howl from one of the dogs for they sounded strangely eerie in the middle of the night. But he sensed that it wasn't that. He lay still in his blankets, cold in the early morning. The air around him was holding its breath, waiting for something to happen. The moon had gone and there was only a faint sprinkling of stars in the sky. There was silence in the village. He guessed it was just before dawn.

A loud noise suddenly screamed through the air, cracking the silence. A noise that Blanco had only heard twice before but which he would have been happy never to have heard again. It was followed by a blazing ball of fire which streaked out of the darkness and crashed into the village. The wooden hut immediately burst into flames.

'The beast!' cried Blanco.

The noise had woken Gump and he sat up, looking completely disorientated. There were shouts from some of the villagers. Blanco could hear Saifullah's voice coming from the house below.

The fire was spreading. The villagers staggered out of their houses, confused, wondering what was going on.

Gump clutched Blanco's arm.

'Look!' he cried.

Lit up by the fire below, they could see miniature flying machines coming in. Blanco knew that each one was filled with firepowder. They didn't do much damage by themselves but the sight of them was terrifying as they popped and whizzed around the heads of the miners.

'How did they get so close with no one seeing them?' asked Blanco, even as he jumped down from the roof. It could only be Count Maleficio and Luca Ferron. No one else had machines like these.

The village was in chaos as the miners raced about, not sure whether to escape from these angry spirits, attack them, or just concentrate on putting out the flames. They were terrified. They didn't know what was causing these fires. The mountain had made her displeasure felt in many ways before—but never like this.

Blanco and Gump tried to help but they were pushed and jostled out of the way and, on one occasion, even kicked. Angry voices shouted at them.

'They're saying the mountain spirits did this,' explained Gump. 'They say it's our fault because we want to take something from her.'

'But this is exactly what we're trying to stop!'

'I know that and you know that,' said Gump, 'but you can't be surprised that they don't realize it.'

'But the villagers far outnumber them. If we could just find the Count and Luca, the villagers could capture them. They can't use the beast and the flying machines close up.'

'Do you want to tell them?'

Blanco looked at the angry and terrified villagers as they threw water on the flames. They were looking for someone to vent their fury on and he had a horrible feeling that it might be him. It probably wasn't the best moment to approach them.

Blanco looked for Saifullah and, catching sight of him, ran over and clutched his arm. Saifullah threw him off, concentrating on directing the miners putting out the flames.

'Please,' cried Blanco. 'I can help you! I can show you where the attackers are. You can stop them!'

Saifullah looked at him with incomprehension and pushed him away. Gump came running over and translated what Blanco said.

'It's evil spirits,' replied Saifullah. 'You have woken the evil spirits. I told you not to ask about the heart-stone.'

'It's not!' pleaded Blanco. 'It's those men I was telling you about.'

But nothing Blanco said made any difference. No matter how hard he and Gump tried to help or explain, they were ignored or cursed.

Eventually Blanco and Gump gave up and stood to one side. The flying machines had stopped coming in and the beast hadn't fired another shot after that first one. It was then that Blanco noticed.

'Where's Faisal?' he said.

Gump looked around. All the miners were racing about with buckets or pots or anything they could fill with water. The darkness had lifted and in the grey half light of dawn they could see who was and wasn't there. And Faisal most definitely was not.

The answer soon became apparent. The fires were out. The villagers were huddled round Saifullah. Accusatory fingers were pointed at Blanco and Gump. Not that they were paying any attention. They were too busy looking around, searching for signs of the Count and Luca Ferron. The beast didn't have a very long range so they couldn't be far away. And if they were close then so was Eva.

The men were approaching Blanco and Gump—but not in a friendly way. Saifullah was trying to reason with them but they didn't seem to be listening. Their fear was louder than his voice—or his authority. Blanco and Gump began to edge backwards. Then the men stopped.

Blanco turned. A party was descending the mountainside. At the front was a triumphant Faisal. In his hands were lit firecrackers. To the astonished miners it looked as though Faisal had captured the power of the evil spirits and cradled them in his hands. All of them, except Saifullah, surged forward, surrounding him. Saifullah stood back, looking thoughtful. He and Gump exchanged worried looks.

Blanco stared at the rest of the group. Count Maleficio and Luca Ferron smiled triumphantly but Blanco barely wasted a glance on them. His eyes quickly sought Eva and he was delighted to see her grinning back and obviously in good health. For the first time since they had left Venice he breathed a sigh of relief.

Eva, despite having been warned not to, ran down the mountainside and threw herself into Blanco's arms. Taken by surprise he stumbled backwards and they fell together in a heap.

'I thought I'd never see you again,' cried Eva, her arms round his neck.

'Didn't you think I'd come after you?' Blanco asked, his voice muffled by Eva's head scarf.

'I hoped you would,' said Eva, 'but we didn't know if you would survive the journey.'

'Well, I did. We did,' he said. 'We all did.'

He jumped to his feet and pulled Eva up behind him.

'What a touching reunion,' beamed Luca Ferron, his cheeks—less rosy and plump after the hardships of the journey—stretching in a smile. Blanco knew better than to think he meant it. He couldn't help noticing how ill Luca looked. His face was a greyish colour and he looked smaller than ever. Maybe it was because he was standing beside Count Maleficio who was so much taller than him but Blanco couldn't help thinking that he had shrunk. The Count was, of course, glaring at him. Blanco gazed at him with interest, seeing that the Count now had scars on both cheeks and his once dazzling silver cloak was dark grey and full of dust. Standing next to him, the Count holding on to her arm, obviously scared that she might follow Eva, was Magdalena. Blanco scowled ferociously at her but she wasn't looking at him. She was looking at Gump, who was talking to Saifullah.

'Well,' said Luca, speaking loudly over the noise the villagers were making, 'here we all are. What a lovely surprise to find you here.'

'There is no heartstone,' said Blanco quickly. 'You've come all this way for nothing.'

'Really?' said Eva, hopefully.

'That's what they told you,' sneered the Count. 'There is a heartstone.'

Blanco turned to Gump and Saifullah. Gump, who had been listening to both conversations, nodded.

'Well, you still can't use Eva . . . ' began Blanco when he was interrupted by a shout.

Faisal was shouting triumphantly. The miners had accepted him as their new leader. He had told them that if they told the strangers where the heartstone lay then the strangers would share the secret of the travelling fire with them. They could use it, not only against their enemies, but also to help them to extract the lapis lazuli. But there was still a lot of shouting going on.

'They are trying to decide whether the loss of the heartstone will compensate for the benefits that the firepowder will bring,' Gump said translating for them all. 'Some think the risk is too great.'

'Tomorrow,' Faisal said, 'we will climb to where the heartstone lies.' He looked at the two groups. 'But not those two,' he said pointing to Eva and Magdalena. 'No women are allowed on the mountain.'

Eva almost shouted with delight.

'Told you so,' said Blanco smugly.

Count Maleficio looked as though he was going to attack Blanco. His grip on his temper seemed more fragile than usual. 'We can't have come all this way and then not use the girl,' he spat. Luca Ferron put up a restraining hand.

'She has to come,' said Luca to Faisal. 'That is part of the deal.'

Faisal looked mutinous. Some of the miners were shaking their heads. They had a muttered discussion.

'Only one of them,' Faisal said eventually.

'That's easy,' said Luca. 'We'll take the girl. The woman can stay with the other two. In fact, you can kill her if you like.'

He cast a malicious look at the Count. Predictably he rose to the teasing.

'No you can't!' he said.

'Relax, my dear Count,' said Luca. 'You can finally have her all to yourself once the old man is dead.'

'No he can't!' said Magdalena.

The Count turned hurt eyes on her. She wrested her arm out of his grip and walked down to stand beside Gump, Blanco, and Eva. The miners were still talking.

'They think there should be some kind of sacrifice to the mountain in return for letting a woman on.'

'I thought I was the sacrifice?' said Eva.

'You're the adept,' said Gump. 'If anyone believes that stupid legend.' Here he paused to glare at the Count. 'It's your role to find the heartstone. The sacrifice they are talking about is to the mountain itself, to appease her for letting women on to the mountain.'

Luca Ferron smiled at that. He turned cold blue eyes on Blanco and Gump and then beckoned to Faisal.

'I can think of a solution to your problem,' said Luca. He turned his cold eyes back on Blanco and Gump. 'They can be your sacrifice. You can kill them.'

'No!' cried Eva, but the men paid her no attention. Blanco grabbed her hand, scared that she was going to attack Luca.

'Don't worry,' he said, although inwardly he was terrified. Now that Saifullah was no longer the leader they had no friends in the village.

Faisal stepped forward, spat on his hand, and shook hands with Luca Ferron. They spoke together for a moment. Count Maleficio stepped forward to do the same, determined not to be left out, although Blanco couldn't help noticing that the Count then wiped his hand surreptitiously on his cloak. The Count also demanded to know what Faisal had said but Luca shook his head impatiently.

'If you were too lazy to learn the language before you came,' he said, 'then I'm not going to waste my time translating every little thing.'

Count Maleficio looked furious but his response was interrupted by one of the miners coming forward with a tray holding an old battered pot and some cups. Faisal handed cups of chai to Luca Ferron and Count Maleficio and they raised them in a toast.

'Shall we lock them up?' Luca asked Faisal.

Faisal shrugged. 'You can if you like,' he said. 'But there is nowhere for them to run anyway. My men will be watching them.'

'Then I think we shall let them enjoy their last days of freedom,' said Luca sweetly.

Chapter 12

'This isn't how it was meant to be,' said Blanco mournfully. He and Eva were sitting on the roof of one of the houses. Two of the villagers were standing below, watching them. They might not have been locked up but they were definitely under guard. 'We were coming to save you, not be captured ourselves.'

'We could run away,' said Eva. 'Tonight.'

Blanco nodded. 'I had thought of that,' he said, 'but they're right when they say they don't need to lock us up. Nobody knows these mountains as well as the villagers. And we have no food. And I think the guards will still be with us through the night.' He paused. 'If only Faisal hadn't managed to persuade the villagers to turn from his father then we could have fought the Count and Luca.'

They both fell silent. Blanco lay back and looked at the first stars which were flickering in the growing darkness. Eva joined him.

'Sometimes,' she said, 'I would look at the stars and wonder what you were doing.'

Blanco laughed nervously. He was too embarrassed to admit that he had sometimes done the same thing. Instead they watched the stars come out together.

* * *

They hadn't gone to find the heartstone the next day. Firstly because Faisal had wanted to try out the fire-powder in the mines before he agreed to anything and secondly because the Count needed time to set up his alchemical furnace. This attracted a lot of attention from the miners who believed that the Count was a great magician who knew the secret of eternal fire. They watched from a safe distance. Some of the small boys would push each other near him and then they would scream and run away when the Count turned round. That was when he noticed them. Most of the time he was fixated on building his laboratory. So he didn't turn round when he felt someone looking at him.

'What are you doing?'

Count Maleficio whirled round at the sound of his second most hated voice. At one time he had thought he hated this man more than anyone else in the world but over the past year that place had been taken by Blanco. He glared at Gump and then turned back to his furnace, determined to ignore him. But Gump was not easily ignored.

'You know that what you are doing is all nonsense. You're just being used.'

Gump had been watching the interplay between the Count and Luca Ferron since they arrived. Luca had not been happy about the Count wanting to set up his furnace but the Count had been adamant, arguing that if they didn't transform the heartstone immediately then it could be stolen or lose some of its power. Luca had eventually agreed but only because Faisal had also wanted more time. It was apparent to everyone except the Count that Luca did not believe that the heartstone was the philosopher's stone. Whatever he wanted it for, it wasn't for the same purpose as the Count.

The Count was furious. 'You seem to forget that I'm the one in charge here,' he said. 'Don't annoy me or we might bring your sacrifice forward.'

Gump looked at the Count and saw that there was no hope of sensible conversation. The Count was completely obsessed with his experiment. For twenty years all he had thought about was getting his revenge on Gump and the future he would have with Magdalena. But Gump decided to give it one more try.

'Leave Blanco and Eva out of this,' he said. 'This is between you and me and Magdalena.'

'But Eva is the adept,' hissed the Count, his silver-grey eyes narrowing. 'Only she can remove the heartstone from its hiding place.'

'Now that bit I definitely made up,' said Gump. 'I'll admit the legend is true—Saifullah's father told me about it when I was here as a boy, but the bit about who could get it out was my invention. It was all a joke.'

The Count didn't find it funny. He had spent the last twenty years of his life trying to break the code that Gump had put in his letters. When the Count, Gump, and Magdalena had all met in Malta twenty years ago Magdalena and Gump had fallen in love but the Count had wanted to marry Magdalena and her father had agreed. Magdalena and Gump made arrangements to elope in coded letters but when Gump discovered that the Count was intercepting the letters he had added the legend about the heartstone to put him off the track. It hadn't worked. The Count had foiled Magdalena and Gump's elopement but Magdalena had still refused to marry the Count. In frustration he had turned back to the letters, determined to find the adept and the heartstone that the legend was about. If the heartstone had magical properties then he could use it to make Magdalena love him. Now Marco Polo was trying to tell him that it was all nonsense—that he had spent half his life on a practical joke. No, he couldn't afford to believe him. The legend had to be true and, as the adept, Eva was going into that mountain.

With a final look of distaste and swirl of his cloak he turned his back on Gump.

Blanco had been avoiding Magdalena. He knew it and she knew it although what she didn't know was why.

'Blanco,' she said, when she could no longer bear it, 'why won't you speak to me?'

'You know why,' he said.

'No. No, I don't. Tell me.'

'I saw you, you know. In Venice.'

'Saw me do what?' Magdalena was truly perplexed.

'Board Luca's ship. The night before Eva was captured.'

Magdalena couldn't help her reaction. She took an involuntary step backwards and covered her mouth with her hand. She couldn't have looked more guilty.

'You see,' said Blanco bitterly. 'You can't deny it. You betrayed Eva.'

He turned and walked away before Magdalena could recover.

'I didn't,' she said. 'I can explain . . . ' But she was already too late.

Blanco and Eva were lying on the roof again. They had snatched every opportunity that they could to be together, trying to think of a way to escape. Blanco was about to tell Eva about Magdalena when they were interrupted by Faisal who jumped on to the roof from the house above, grabbed Blanco by the arm and tried to drag him off.

'Let me go!' cried Blanco.

'Let him go!' added Eva, hitting Faisal ineffectually on his back.

Despite Blanco's best efforts Faisal pulled him off the roof quite easily. He threw him into the nearest house and then barred the door. Eva flew at it but Faisal pulled her away.

'Leave it,' said a voice from behind them. It was Luca Ferron.

'Don't try to set him free,' he said, 'or we will kill him outright. And get a good night's sleep. We leave tomorrow.'

'Well, this isn't quite how I imagined the great reunion,' said Blanco glumly. 'I barely even saw her. And now I'll never see her again. I'll never see anyone again.'

Gump had been thrown into the house moments after Blanco. While Blanco had been relieved to see him, he also knew that this meant that the time for their sacrifice was probably near. To think he had always been worried about Eva being the sacrifice and now it turned out to be him as well. Eva had to take the risk of retrieving the heartstone but ironically Blanco was the sacrifice that would allow her on to the mountain in the first place.

'There's no need to panic,' said Gump calmly. 'We'll get out of this.'

'How?' asked Blanco. 'We're surrounded by miners who want to sacrifice us. Even if we escape them we have two men who want to kill us, and they have quite a number of men in their pay who would be happy to do it for them.'

'Blanco.'

It was faint but quite unmistakable.

'Eva?'

'Blanco.'

There it was again, followed this time by a faint tapping sound.

He followed the sound and found that it was coming from the far wall.

'Eva!' he hissed.

The tapping stopped. She must be in the house next door. All the houses were connected, usually only by a thin wall.

'Blanco,' she said. 'Are you all right?'

'As well as can be expected for someone who's going to die in the morning.'

He heard Gump snort with derision in the corner.

'We'll get you out,' she said. 'The angels will do something.'

Blanco was slightly comforted by that. But he was more worried about Eva.

'The angels should go with you,' he said firmly.

'They are supposed to protect you. Gump and I can look after ourselves.'

Gump snorted again. They didn't seem to be doing too well so far.

There was silence.

'Blanco,' said Eva quietly. 'I'm scared.'

Blanco cursed the wooden wall which stood between them. All he could say was what he had said before. 'I won't let them hurt you,' he said. 'I'll be there before you have to go into the mountain.'

'Someone's coming!' said Eva. And with that she was gone. Perhaps for the last time.

'You have to stay and get him out,' said Micha.

'I thought you said I shouldn't interfere,' said Azaz.

'I've changed my mind.'

'I'll help you.'

They both turned to find Rameel behind. Azaz laughed scornfully.

'Why would we need your help?' asked Micha.

Azaz stared at him suspiciously.

'And why would you want to help?' he asked.

Rameel shrugged. 'I think he should be there at the end,' he said. 'He was there at the beginning.'

The truth was, although he would never admit it, the dark angel couldn't bear to see Eva's tears.

When Blanco and Gump were brought out of the house they found Magdalena outside. She looked petrified

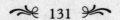

and Gump went to comfort her but was stopped by one of the miners.

'Has she gone?' he asked Magdalena.

Magdalena nodded her head. 'They came for her a short time ago, as soon as the sun started to rise.'

Blanco looked around. Faisal was sneering. So he hadn't gone with the others. He had obviously just told them where to find the heartstone.

'Prepare yourself,' muttered Blanco to Gump and Magdalena.

'For what?' asked Gump.

A moment later he looked terrified as he rose into the air.

'That,' said Blanco with a grin as he also started levitating. He had seen Azaz behind him and he could see very faint outlines of two other figures behind Gump and Magdalena. Two, he thought briefly. Does that mean that Rameel is helping?

Magdalena joined them a moment later.

The miners backed off and started shouting amongst themselves. Faisal was pale and quite obviously terrified. The sacrifice wasn't meant to happen like this. What kind of strange magic did these strangers have at their control?

All three were now hovering above the heads of the miners.

The men were shouting at Faisal but he could do nothing except stare in terror. Then he turned and ran. The others jeered and one threw a clod of earth after him. At the end of the village a door opened and Saifullah came out. He looked shocked when he saw his guests suspended in the air but he quickly recovered his wits.

'How are you doing that, old friend?' he asked, coming to a stop before Gump.

'You have your spirits of the mountain,' replied Gump as calmly as he could, given that he wasn't entirely sure himself. He couldn't see anyone holding him but he could feel strong arms around him. 'We have our own. They want to save us from being killed.'

Saifullah nodded and turning back to the miners barked out some orders. They hesitated for a moment but they were much more used to obeying Saifullah than Faisal and they quickly dispersed.

'Come down,' said Saifullah. 'The men won't hurt you now.'

Slowly Blanco, Gump, and Magdalena were lowered to the ground.

'Can you tell us where the heartstone is?' demanded Blanco as soon as he was on his feet. He looked pleadingly at Saifullah. 'Faisal told the others where to go. They'll force Eva to go in and get the heartstone.'

Saifullah frowned at that.

'You can't send a woman into the mountain,' he said. 'She will be furious. She'll shake and destroy us all.'

'So help us,' said Gump. 'Help us to reach there before they send her in.'

'I know a shortcut,' said Saifullah. 'It's steep but you should get there in time.'

Chapter 13

They were only just in time. The angels flew on ahead to make sure the path was clear but it still took them longer than they had hoped. By the time they reached the plateau Blanco could see that the Count and Luca were trying to force Eva to enter the mine.

'Let her go!' cried Blanco, running towards them.

Eva was delighted to see him. She thought she had been abandoned. No Blanco. No angels. But now they were all here. She could see the angels hovering overhead and her heart lightened. She couldn't be forced into the mountain now.

The Count had never been more angry in his life. Every step of the journey, Blanco had dogged him and disrupted things at the last moment. Nothing had ever gone to plan and he hated it when things didn't go according to plan. He didn't spend months laying schemes to have some boy come and ruin them.

As Blanco ran past him to reach Eva, Count Maleficio stuck out a leg and tripped him. Blanco landed with a thump but before he could scramble to his feet the Count was on him and had a knife against his throat.

'Send the girl in,' he hissed at Luca Ferron. 'Send her in and don't anyone else move or I will cut his throat.'

His silver-grey eyes glittered in an unpredictable way and Blanco was terrified that he might get his throat cut whether Eva went in to the mountain or not.

The angels hung overhead uselessly.

'Rameel?' said Azaz. 'If we . . . '

'No,' said Rameel.

Azaz frowned. 'I thought you were working with us now,' he said.

'You thought wrong,' said Rameel. 'You know I only do what suits me.'

Azaz cast a look at Micha, as if to say, I told you so.

Micha knew that Rameel had grown fond of Eva during the travels. She was sure that was why he had offered to free Blanco.

'We need to protect Eva,' she said.

'No,' said Rameel firmly. 'She has to go in. She has to get the heartstone. If you try to stop her then Blanco will die.'

Eva had heard enough.

'Where is it?'

'Eva! No!' said Blanco. 'You don't have to do it!'

She looked straight into his eyes. She knew that Blanco would go into the mountain for her and so she would do it for him. After all, he had come halfway round the world in search of her. And she didn't have to give the heartstone to the others when she came out.

'Yes I do,' she said.

Luca Ferron cut in.

'Here's some firepowder,' he said.

'What!?'

The exclamation came from both Gump and Blanco. Nobody had mentioned firepowder before.

'The heartstone may be hidden behind a rock wall,' continued Luca Ferron calmly. 'The only way in may be to blow it up. Why do you think we brought it all this way?' He turned to Blanco. 'You'd better tell her the best way to use this stuff.'

'No,' said Blanco. 'I'm not telling her how to blow herself up. An explosion underground could bring the whole mountain down.'

He wished he could bite his words back as soon as he said them for Eva looked terrified again.

'If you don't tell her,' said Luca, 'then Maleficio will. Who do you trust more to get it right?'

'How dare you?' the Count spat out. 'I was the one who invented the beast!'

'Yes, but I was the one who actually got it to work,' said Blanco.

The Count had struggled with the beast for weeks on Malta before Blanco had discovered how to make it work properly.

The scars on the Count's cheeks flared scarlet at the reminder and he pressed the knife harder against Blanco's throat.

'Let me up,' Blanco said to the Count calmly.

Count Maleficio shook his head. He was taking absolutely no chances this time. Every time he had given Blanco the smallest chance in the past he had escaped. But now they were too close to their final destination for him to risk anything.

'Tell the girl what she needs to know,' he snarled, his desire for the stone greater than his pride.

Sighing, Blanco looked at Eva and slowly explained how the mixture should be put together.

'Do you understand?' he said finally. 'You must not add the saltpetre until the charcoal and sulphur are mixed. And only a little bit. No bigger than your fingernail.'

She nodded reluctantly.

'But if you don't want to do it, don't do it,' he said urgently. 'I'll be fine.'

Eva smiled weakly at that. Only Blanco could say that when he had a knife held against his throat.

She looked round the group. The Count and Luca Ferron she barely glanced at. She looked for longer at Magdalena and Gump. She smiled at them, a sweet smile that made Gump furious with himself for putting her in so much danger. If only he had never written those letters none of this would be happening. Magdalena started to cry and he put his arm around her.

Azaz and Micha could only watch helplessly. They knew what lay within the mountain but they were forbidden to say. They were also forbidden to follow her in.

Rameel, nervous, sat by the entrance, pulling at the feathers on his wings.

Eva looked at Azaz and Micha and blew them a kiss.

Azaz nodded firmly at her. 'Come back,' was all he said.

'Be careful,' said Micha.

Finally Eva's gaze settled on Blanco. Green eyes looked into brown and all the adventures they had shared since they met were in that look. It seemed a lifetime ago that she had first spoken to him on the *Santa Maria*, the ship travelling to Barcelona from Venice. They had been through a lot since then, both together and apart. This was just one more adventure.

'Eva,' he said. 'You don't have to go. I'd rather die than put you in danger.'

She smiled and he was reminded of the first time he had ever seen her. He closed his eyes briefly to remember it better and when he opened them she was gone.

Within moments Eva was shrouded in darkness. She considered lighting the candle that she had with her but she knew she would find it difficult to crawl with only one hand. Anyway, it wasn't as though she could get lost. There was only one way to go. Feeling her way she continued forward, trying to ignore the fear that was gnawing away at her stomach. It travelled to her bones, causing her legs and arms to feel weird and shaky. Trembling, she reached out a hand and started crawling forward.

Looking over her shoulder she could see the tiny pinprick of light from the entrance fade to nothing. Now she really was in the dark. She sat back on her heels for a moment, trying to control her breathing which sounded loud and harsh as it bounced off the walls. For a moment she thought she could hear something else breathing as well but she soon realized that it was just her own echo. She tried to ignore the sound and started to move forward again. Soon she found she could stand up. Carefully, keeping one hand on the wall, she did so and carried on.

Azaz was watching Rameel. He had never seen him so agitated. He kept glancing at Luca Ferron who was sitting on a rock, calmly watching the entrance. Azaz glanced between the two and a shocking thought suddenly occurred to him. He flew over to Micha and whispered in her ear. She, looking horrified, glanced at the two. She turned back to Azaz and this time when they both looked at Luca Ferron he smiled at them. It chilled them completely.

'423 . . . 424 . . . 425 . . . ' Eva was counting her steps, trying to ignore the fact that the blood was pumping loudly in her ears. She wanted to cry but knew if she started she might never stop. A feeling of panic rippled through her and she stopped for a moment to try to control her fear.

'Breathe,' she told herself. 'Breathe.'

She took a deep breath and thought of Blanco. The thought of him made her keep going. Having the heartstone was the only thing that would stop the Count from killing him.

Magdalena was trying to reason with the Count but he wouldn't listen to her. He was completely fixated on the idea that the heartstone was nearly in his hands. With the power that it would give him, he could sort out everything. He would make gold and live for ever. And, with both those things, he would make Magdalena love him.

'I don't need you to bargain for me,' said Blanco. He still hadn't forgiven her for betraying Eva back in Venice.

'I think you do,' said Gump mildly. His calm tone completely belied the panic that he felt at the sight of Blanco in such danger. He had never been a violent man but he wanted to punch the Count. Hard. Surely there was something he could do?

'You betrayed Eva,' said Blanco, looking at her fiercely.

'I didn't.'

Blanco stared at her angrily. How could she have forgotten? Betrayal wasn't something that could be done lightly so how could she have forgotten? Did she have so little feeling for Eva?

'What were you doing on the ship then?'

'I was trying to save you.'

Just as Eva thought she couldn't go any further she walked straight into a wall. Cursing and rubbing her sore head, she fumbled about in her pack and found the candle and a flint. Striking the flint on the wall, she lit the candle and found herself surrounded by blank rock faces on three sides. This was the place then. She took out the ingredients that Blanco had directed her to make up. Now she had to mix the right quantities. She could only pray that she remembered it properly, that it would work, and that the tunnel was strong enough to hold. She was tempted to run back outside and say there was nothing there but she knew that they wouldn't believe her and would make her go back in. And the Count would kill Blanco. He had been longing to do it for months. The heartstone was his only chance. She held her candle up and looked round the walls again. They seemed fairly strong and solid. Surely they could withstand a small explosion?

Taking a deep breath she lit the mixture and then ran back along the tunnel as far as she could. She wasn't very far away when she heard the bang. Trembling she put a hand on the wall and waited to see what collapsed. The wall vibrated with the explosion but seemed to be holding. The only problem was that up ahead, where the explosion had been, there was a huge cloud of smoke and dust. Sitting down, Eva waited for it to clear.

Lifting her head from her knees, Eva noticed that the smoke was growing less. Coughing, she crawled forward through the smoke, staying low where the air was clearer. She crawled all the way to the far wall to see if the firepowder had worked.

At first she thought it hadn't. The wall looked just as solid as before. But as the smoke and dust began to settle she found there was a hole at the base of the wall, just big enough for her to scramble through. It was a tight squeeze and she wasn't sure what, if anything, she was going to find on the other side. But after a few moments she felt clear space above her head. A moment later she had enough space to stand up. She lit her candle again.

Eva knew from what Saifullah had told her, that lapis lazuli was cut out of the mountain and usually looked like white or grey rock until it was filed and polished. But this one was just embedded in the far wall, already polished, just waiting to be pulled out.

Even by the light of one candle it glistened as she approached. She was almost scared to touch it. Was this really someone's heart? She crouched down to get a better look and then reached out a hand.

'What do you mean, save me?' asked Blanco.

'I did go on to their ship,' said Magdalena, glancing first at Gump and then at Blanco. 'I was trying to persuade Christobal, I mean the Count, that the whole thing was just a joke that your great-uncle and I had made up. I thought that he would believe me even though he didn't believe anyone else. But he didn't.'

'You always lied to me,' said the Count, finally shifting his gaze from Blanco to Magdalena. 'And this proves it. There *is* a stone.'

'But it's not the philosopher's stone,' she said. 'It won't do what you want, Christobal. It won't give you eternal life. It won't turn metal into gold. And most of all it won't make me love you. The others are just using you.'

The Count looked stricken and tightened his hold on the knife. Behind her, Luca raised an amused eyebrow.

Magdalena looked at Blanco.

'How could I betray her?' she asked. 'Quite apart

from loving her like a daughter I didn't know where we were going to be that day. I didn't know about the wedding or the fact that you would save her or that we would end up in Bartolommeo's shop.'

Blanco had to admit that what she said was true and he bit his lip. Had he been wrong after all?

'I hate to say it,' said Gump, 'but I told you so. Actually,' he continued, 'I don't hate saying so. It's always nice to be proved right and anyone who says otherwise is a liar.'

'So you didn't believe I had betrayed her,' she said, smiling at Gump.

'Of course not.'

The Count had noticed her smile and he turned to glare at his rival, his attention momentarily diverted from Blanco. It was all the chance that Blanco needed. With a great effort he pushed the Count off him and jumped to his feet before the Count realized what had happened.

Blanco ran, his eyes fixed determinedly on the small opening.

He almost made it. He was just about there when he heard a cry of rage. He sprinted faster but just as he dived into the entrance a hand clutched hold of his ankle and started dragging him backwards.

Chapter 14

It fell into her hands. Eva hadn't expected it to happen so easily and she almost dropped it. She only just managed to catch it before it fell on the floor. It was cool to the touch, smooth but with sharp edges. As she held it in her hands it began to warm up and she could feel an energy emanating from it. She sank down against the wall and looked at it. There were little golden sparks deep within it. Eva could have sworn they were moving.

'Do you have any idea of the trouble you have caused?' she said out loud.

'*Yes.*'

Eva looked round in shock and then laughed at herself. It was because she was sitting in the dark. It made her imagine things.

'So many people looking for you,' she said, stroking its smooth surface, 'and why?'

The stone seemed to get warmer as she spoke which made her stop. In the silence that followed there was no doubting the voice this time.

'*Thank you for setting me free.*'

'Who are you?' asked Eva, only a little bit scared. 'Are you an angel?'

Laughter filled the air. '*Don't talk to me of angels. It was an angel who put me in here. No, I'm definitely not an angel.*'

Eva knew from the legend that an angel had buried the heartstone in the mountain.

'You're the girl!' she said in surprise. 'Who loved someone else. Not the angel.'

'That's me.'

'You must hate him,' said Eva.

'Not any more. I have forgiven him.'

'Have you?' asked Eva in shock. She didn't think that she could ever forgive anyone for trapping her inside a mountain for centuries.

'There is no time any more for hatred or bitterness or regrets. I wasted centuries on that. Now I'm free. I can go to the one I love. So why not forgive the angel? Will you tell him?'

'I don't know who he is.'

'Didn't he send you here? To set me free?'

Eva was confused. 'I-I'm not sure,' she said.

'Do you love someone?'

Eva smiled. 'Yes,' she said.

'Does he love you?'

Eva stopped smiling. 'I don't know,' she said. 'But he did follow me around the world,' she added quickly.

The spirit laughed. *'You know if he does. You always know.'*

Eva was used to talking to her angels and so she wasn't nearly as terrified as she could have been at talking to a disembodied voice but one thing was making her feel queasy.

'This isn't actually your heart I'm holding, is it?'

The laughter pealed out again. *'No. It's the emotions from that time. It's the key that was locking me in place. But now, I'm free. Thanks to you. Maybe my forgiveness will free us all.'*

'Has it got any power? There are men outside who think it holds the secret to eternal life or gold or something. They think . . . '

'*Power is never what it seems. The stone will change depending on who is holding it.*'

Eva could feel the stone begin to turn icy cold. A loud crack echoed across the chamber.

'*Go,*' said the spirit, her voice changing. '*Go! The tunnel is collapsing. Now that you have removed the stone there is nothing holding it up. Go!*'

'What about you?'

'*I am free. I can go wherever I like. But you must run or you will have to take my place.*'

Eva ran.

She was crouching down trying to get back through the narrowest part of the tunnel when it happened. As she was wriggling her way through, the tunnel collapsed, crushing her to the floor. Her arms, which had been stretched out in front of her, were free, as were her head and chest. But the rest of her, from the waist down, was trapped. It only took a few moments for Eva to realize that, although she seemed to be unhurt, she was doomed. No one else could come in after her because the Count and Luca believed that only she was allowed in. She would be left here to die. She couldn't see anything through the darkness, not a single glimmer of light, not a sound from the spirit. As she lay there the air around her seemed to darken and grow heavy and she could hear loud harsh breathing. She couldn't help herself. She screamed.

* * *

Blanco felt himself being dragged backwards and he kicked out. It was to no avail. As he was drawn back into sunlight he turned to face the evil eyes of Count Maleficio.

Rameel was now hovering disconsolately over the entrance to the mine. He flew over to the Count and Blanco, desperate to hear if Blanco had heard or seen anything in the brief moments that he had been inside. Azaz was huddled with Micha, talking over what they should do when Eva came out with the heartstone. They kept glancing towards Luca Ferron. He was ignoring everyone else and was staring fixedly at the entrance to the tunnel. He was determined that only he would get the stone.

The Count had had enough.

'This is it, boy!' he screamed. 'This time I really am going to kill you!' With a cry of rage he aimed his knife straight for Blanco's heart.

At the same moment Azaz made a dash for the tunnel entrance.

'Azaz!' cried Micha. 'No!'

Rameel saw where he was going and raced after him but he was too late. Azaz had disappeared inside.

Micha dashed after him but Rameel caught her before she went inside.

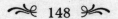

'No, Micha,' he said, and for once he wasn't thinking of himself. 'You can't go in.'

Micha struggled ineffectually in his arms but eventually slumped against him. Where Azaz had gone, she knew she couldn't follow. Angels couldn't breathe underground and to follow wouldn't help either of them.

Blanco saw the knife with startling clarity and for a moment everything happened in slow motion. The knife descended at the same time as he caught a movement out of the corner of his eye. He threw up his arm to defend himself but it was thrust aside by the Count's downward momentum. Then he crashed on to his back, winded. The Count was staggering back, knife no longer in his hand, but with a horrified look on his face. Magdalena was between them. As Blanco watched she clutched herself around the middle and blood began to seep through her fingers. He could see the handle of the knife lodged there. Her face was shocked and she staggered. Gump ran over, catching her as she fell. She clutched at him desperately as her eyes closed and he laid her gently on the ground. Count Maleficio was horrified at what he had done and could only stare hopelessly at her crumpled form.

'Eva!'

Eva thought she was dreaming. The darkness was still pressing in on her and she was sure that she was imagining things. She couldn't be hearing Azaz's voice. Blanco's maybe. Or Gump's. She would even have welcomed the sound of Luca Ferron's voice, although she was fairly sure that he would just take the heartstone and leave her behind. But she couldn't be hearing Azaz because angels were forbidden to go underground. Micha had explained it to her on Malta. They were creatures of the air and too much earth was bad for them. It suffocated them.

So, it was only by some cruel trick that it was Azaz's voice she could hear. She closed her eyes.

'Eva!'

She heard it again, quite insistent this time. A moment later she felt fingers against her forehead, brushing her hair away from her eyes. Her eyes flew open.

'Azaz?'

Surely she was still dreaming.

'Ouch! What did you do that for?'

Azaz had pinched her.

'Just checking you were still alive,' he said cheerily. Much more cheerily than he felt, for already he could feel his breathing slowing. He would have to act quickly.

'My legs are completely trapped,' she said. 'I don't think they're hurt but I can't move them to find out.'

Azaz was feeling around the broken rubble to see how much of the stone was covering Eva's legs. His wings were moving gently back and forwards giving Eva some much needed cool air. He thought that he could get her out although it would be difficult. He started to lift off the stones. Eva wasn't so much crushed as trapped, unable to twist her body round to free herself.

Eva could feel the weight lifting as Azaz removed the stones.

'Azaz,' she said. 'You haven't even asked me if I found the heartstone.'

'*I know that you did.*'

'How did you know?'

'*I could tell by Rameel's reactions.*'

'What does Rameel have to do with it?'

'*More than you know.*'

'Then tell me.

'*Let's get you out of here first.*'

Blanco knew there was nothing he could do for Magdalena that Gump couldn't do better. While the Count was still stunned by what he had just done Blanco took his chance. He ran to the entrance to the mine. This time no one stopped him.

As he crawled along the passageway he wondered how far into the mountain he would have to travel. He raced ahead. Sooner than he expected he heard voices and knew that Azaz and Eva must be near.

He couldn't see anything but they weren't difficult to find. As Eva had discovered earlier, there was only one tunnel, which made it impossible to get lost.

He was crawling along when his hand suddenly touched flesh. It was hard to tell who screamed the loudest—Blanco or Eva. His eardrums throbbed, and Azaz, who had sensed Blanco's arrival, wished that he had said something earlier. He was just lifting the last of the rocks from Eva's legs and Eva, in her surprise, had kicked him.

'*It's only Blanco,*' said Azaz, a little crossly, rubbing his wing where her foot had made contact. His breathing was getting slower.

'What was that?' said Blanco, still shaken from touching something human when he was expecting rock.

'My hand,' said Eva, scrambling forward to greet him. 'I was on the floor. Azaz has just freed me. Come on. Let's go.'

'Hold on!' said both Blanco and Azaz.

Blanco wasn't sure that they should just rush outside and hand over the heartstone. He wanted to talk it over first to see if they could come up with a plan.

'Blanco,' said Azaz. *'Could you come here?'*

Blanco squeezed past Eva to where the angel was. With his huge height he was only half standing, his back against the ceiling of the tunnel. Blanco could only make this out because of the faint glow from Azaz's golden belt. Otherwise all was darkness.

'Blanco,' said Azaz quietly into Blanco's ear. *'You must take Eva and go immediately.'*

'But . . . ' said Blanco.

'Now,' said Azaz.

His tone brooked no argument and the urgency in it transferred to Blanco. Azaz whispered something in Blanco's ear and Blanco nodded reluctantly and stepped away from the angel.

'Eva, we should go,' he said.

'That's what I said,' said Eva petulantly. 'It was you two who stopped me, but now that you think we can go, then . . . '

'Shut up, Eva,' said Blanco, 'and start moving.'

He could hear a sound behind him, a sound that he didn't like. It was a loud crack.

'Don't tell me to shut up! I've just been talking to a ghost and been caught in a rock fall!'

Blanco ignored her and pushed her along in front of him. At first she tried to protest but as the cracking sound got louder she understood the sense of urgency and moved faster. When they reached the lower part they both got down on their hands and knees and rushed as fast as they could.

'Azaz!' shouted Eva, halting at one point near the end. 'You must be finding this a tight squeeze!'

There was no reply. Just an onward push from Blanco. But Eva had stopped.

'Azaz!' she called again.

Nothing.

'Keep going!' called Blanco, pushing her.

The noise behind them had lessened but Blanco suspected he knew why and he also suspected that the drop in sound wouldn't last for very long.

'Where is he?' cried Eva, trying to turn round and finding it impossible in the small space. 'We have to go back. We have to find him.'

Blanco tried to push her forward again.

'Eva,' he said, 'we have to get out. The whole tunnel's going to collapse.'

'But Azaz . . . '

'Azaz is holding it up,' said Blanco. 'We'd have been buried back there if he wasn't. And he's holding it up for you, Eva, so you've got to keep moving. Please.'

For another few moments Eva didn't move. Just when Blanco thought that they were going to be stuck for ever she started crawling forward.

While they were still some distance from the entrance, Blanco could sense Eva turning round to face him.

'We have to go back,' she said.

But only a moment later, there was an almighty crack. A great whooshing sound accompanied it and Blanco knew that they were about to be enveloped in a cloud of dust and stone. He shoved Eva towards the light—and more danger.

Chapter 15

Micha and Rameel were hovering outside the entrance. The first sign that something was wrong was when a cloud of greyish ash came billowing out. It smelt strongly of sulphur. Then Blanco stumbled out, dragging a crying Eva behind him. Once out, she pulled her hand from Blanco's, ran a few steps and collapsed on the ground.

'What is it?' said Micha, hovering over Eva. 'What's happened?'

'Did you get it?' asked Rameel.

Eva ignored them both and continued to cry.

Micha looked at Blanco but he refused to catch her eye.

'Where's Az . . . ' she began.

As she spoke a loud crack sounded, followed by a series of crashes which grew louder and louder. As they watched, a huge wall of ash billowed out of the tunnel and then it all collapsed, destroying the entrance.

Eva curled herself into a ball and wouldn't say anything so everyone turned to Blanco.

'What happened in there?' demanded Luca Ferron.

Blanco crouched down next to Eva. He stroked her hair gently.

'Eva,' he began.

'Go away,' she said. 'I don't want to talk to you. It's all your fault.'

'*What's all his fault?*' *asked Micha.* '*Where's Azaz?*'

For the first time Blanco could see Micha clearly. She was only a little smaller than Azaz and she had a bright golden face and hair the same colour as Eva's. Her wings had the same golden glow as her face but at the moment they sagged heavily against her back, looking as forlorn as her face. Blanco said nothing but his involuntary glance towards the mine was enough for Micha. Slowly she allowed herself to float back down to earth and sank to her knees next to Eva.

'*Eva!*' *She shook Eva angrily by the shoulder.* '*Eva! Tell me you didn't leave Azaz in there!*'

'It's not Eva's fault!' cried Blanco. 'It wasn't anyone's fault! He told us to go.'

Luca Ferron tried to pull Eva to her feet but she resisted him.

'Where is it?' he demanded harshly. 'Did you get it?'

Eva continued to cry. He shook her.

'Leave her alone!' shouted Blanco.

'Did she get it?'

Blanco shrugged his shoulders.

'I don't know,' he said. 'She was already on her way out when I met her.'

Their argument was interrupted by a howl of despair. Micha had realized that Azaz was not coming back out of the mine. Screaming, she shot straight up into the air and disappeared.

They stood round in a little half circle. Count Maleficio, Gump, Luca Ferron, Blanco, and Eva with Rameel circling above their heads. There was silence. No one knew what to do or say next. Gump walked back over to Magdalena. She was leaning against a rock. She looked pale and her eyes were shut. She opened them at Gump's return and gave him a faint smile. She saw that Eva had returned and relief swept through her.

Luca had released Eva. She looked round at them all. They were staring at her. Involuntarily her hand slipped to her pocket and Luca Ferron's eyes lit up with glee as he realized that she had, after all, got the heartstone. He stepped towards her.

Only to find Blanco in his way.

'Get out of my way, boy,' he growled, any pretence at humour or civility completely gone from his voice.

They were both surprised when a soft voice came from behind Blanco.

'Don't you know,' said Eva, 'that only the person who takes it out can use it.'

'That's nonsense!' said Count Maleficio, also coming forward. 'It doesn't say that anywhere.'

'I know because it told me,' continued Eva dreamily. She didn't seem to be completely present. She seemed to be growing fainter as they looked at her.

'Eva!'

Blanco grabbed her arm, feeling as he did so as though he were pulling her back to earth. Eva shook her head. For a moment it had felt as if the spirit had tried to take her away. She curled her hand round the stone. It was still icy cold.

The Count and Luca Ferron both took another step nearer.

'She's right,' Blanco said. 'That's what the prophet said as well.'

'What prophet?'

'At the Minaret of Jam. He said that only the one who brought the heartstone out could use it.'

Blanco also knew now what the prophet had meant about a sacrifice being made out of love. Azaz had sacrificed himself for Eva. Blanco could never have held the tunnel up. Only Azaz could have done that.

Blanco could see that Count Maleficio and Luca Ferron wanted to snatch the stone from Eva but they didn't know whether she spoke the truth. It was enough to make them both pause. Nobody liked to gainsay a prophecy.

'I can tell her what to do,' said the Count eagerly. 'Once she's made the potion, you can both go free.'

'Do you think I'm a fool?' Eva demanded of the Count. 'Do you really think I believe that you would set me free? No, the stone stays with me.'

'What potion?' asked Blanco.

'He thinks this is the philosopher's stone,' said Eva, still not looking directly at Blanco. 'He thinks it will make him live for ever. He thinks it will make Magdalena love him and they will live together for ever. But it's not.'

From where he sat with Magdalena, Gump let out a snort. The Count glared at him.

'I don't believe you,' he said.

Eva caught sight of Magdalena.

'What happened?' she asked.

She tried to run over to Magdalena but both Luca Ferron and Count Maleficio blocked her way.

'It was my fault!' cried the Count. 'I might have killed her! Don't you see? That's why we have to use the stone. We can bring her back to life! You could save her!'

Eva paused. If it was the philosopher's stone and it could bring eternal life then maybe it could be used to save Magdalena. Whatever else could be said about the Count, he really loved Magdalena. Or, at least, what he thought was love. Her fingers closed around the stone. It seemed to be getting warmer and warmer as she held it, soaking up her energy. The iciness that she had felt in the chamber had disappeared.

'I don't believe you,' she said hesitantly.

'I've had enough of this,' interrupted Luca Ferron. 'He's talking rubbish. Alchemy is not a matter of a moment. It is a process of transformation. Even if it was the philosopher's stone it would take months to get it to work. You'd never save her in time. Give *me* the stone.'

'No,' said Eva fiercely. 'It's mine.'

Rameel had been hovering overhead while all this was going on. With Azaz trapped in the tunnel and Micha having disappeared no one could stop him getting what he wanted.

Unseen by the others, Luca Ferron slipped a small knife out of his pocket. He edged over towards the Count. The Count's eyes were fixed on the stone still firmly clutched in Eva's hand. She had drawn it out of her pocket and he could see it gleaming through her fingers. He had a determined glint in his eye. He was convinced that the stone would make Magdalena love him. For the last twenty years he had been consumed with the idea of making Magdalena love him and the stone had been a crucial part of that obsession. He couldn't let it disappear now.

Luca had another plan altogether. He had never admitted why he wanted the stone. The Count had always assumed that it was for the same reason as him—to live for ever and have incalculable wealth. But Luca knew that the heartstone wasn't the philosopher's stone. It was exactly what the legend said it was. It was a heart that had been buried thousands of years ago. It wasn't the actual heart, of course, but it was all the love and passion, all the feelings that make up a human heart. It was sealed tight with the strong emotions of jealousy and hatred and that was why it looked like an eye filmed with tears. But it was the only thing on earth that could give Luca what he wanted. It was the only thing that could turn him into an angel again.

Rameel was waiting for his chance. He just needed Eva to open her hand slightly and he could reach in and snatch the stone. He hadn't guided, cajoled, and encouraged the Count and Luca Ferron all this way for them to get the stone. He wanted it for himself. It was his by right and no one was going to stop him.

Eva watched as the Count and Luca both approached her. She was also vaguely aware that the dark angel Rameel was hovering above her and she wondered whose side he was on. Blanco put his arm around her so that she knew he was right there with her. It felt strangely comforting but they were still only two against three. Gump left Magdalena and came and stood beside them. Now they were three against three. She didn't have to give them the stone any more. No one was holding a blade to Blanco's throat. No one could make her do anything.

'Come now,' said Luca with a smile. 'I'm sure we can come to some kind of amicable agreement.' His face was grey and he stumbled as he walked.

'There's one thing I could do with it,' said Eva.

'What?' cried Count Maleficio and Luca Ferron together.

'I could smash it.'

She held it out in the palm of her hand, balanced squarely in the middle. Despite the density of its colour, it pulsated with light. It was a deep, indigo blue—the colour of the middle of the night. Red tones glowed deep within it, drinking in the sunlight. There were a few gold stars which winked as they caught the light. They were darting about within the stone, tiny pulses of energy.

'No!'

They both shouted.

Rameel had heard and seen enough. He couldn't risk someone else taking the stone but even more than that he couldn't risk it being smashed. Flying down, he knocked Eva off her feet and, as she fell, snatched the stone from her grasp.

'Well done, Rameel!' called Luca, looking pleased. 'Now bring the stone to me.'

Count Maleficio cast an incredulous look at Luca Ferron.

'I don't think so,' he said. 'Rameel, give it to me.'

Rameel looked from one to the other with a look of absolute scorn on his face.

'*Why would I give it to either of you?*' he asked. '*It's mine.*'

His white face was tense and he clutched the stone tightly to his breast.

'But we've been working together,' said Luca. 'We started this together and then we let Maleficio join us. But we were the ones who began it all.'

'That's not true!' cried the Count. 'Rameel and I started this together and then you came along.'

Rameel rolled his eyes.

'*I wasn't working with either of you,*' he said. '*I was getting both of you to do what I wanted. I want the stone for myself.*'

'Rameel, you don't need the stone,' whined the Count. 'You have eternal life and you don't need any gold. Give it to me.'

'*This isn't the philosopher's stone, you fool!*'

'But you said it was.'

'*I lied.*'

'So give it to me,' said Luca.

'*No.*'

Luca looked desperate. He seemed to be ageing in front of their eyes. His skin was growing increasingly grey and he was stooping more than before. He narrowed his eyes at Rameel and raised a hand.

Rameel looked alarmed. He took a few steps backwards and then rose into the air. With a final glance at Eva, he flew off.

'I don't understand,' said Blanco, 'why would Rameel want the stone?'

Micha had slowly come back down to earth as Rameel had been talking.

'Isn't it obvious?' she asked. 'Haven't you guessed by now?'

They all looked at her questioningly.

'It's his,' she said to the astonished group. 'He's the angel from the legend. He's the one who buried it in the first place.'

'Nooo!'

Luca's cry when it came was shockingly loud. He screamed up at the sky, shaking his fists in futile fury. Then he raced off in the same direction as Rameel. After a moment's hesitation, the Count followed him.

Chapter 16

'I have a feeling that this isn't over yet,' said Blanco. He looked over at Micha. Golden tears slipped from her eyes.

'You're right,' said Micha. *She was sitting on the rubble at the opening of the mine where Azaz was still trapped.* *'You have to get the stone back.'*

Eva tried to put her arm around Micha but Micha drew back. Eva looked hurt so Blanco put his arm around her. She was feeling very upset about Azaz but she knew they had to get the stone back. Azaz always managed to get himself out of difficult situations so why should this time be any different? Eva wanted to tell Micha this but she didn't know how.

'Why?' asked Blanco.

'You can't risk Luca Ferron getting the stone,' Micha said. *'Azaz and I were going to stop him but now you must do it.'*

'Why him in particular?' asked Blanco. 'What about the Count?'

Micha shrugged. *'The Count doesn't matter,'* she said. *'What the others said to him is true. The heartstone is not the philosopher's stone. It will do nothing for him. But you must stop Luca.'*

'Come with us,' said Blanco. 'Help us to stop him.'

Micha shook her head. *'No,'* she said. *'I won't leave Azaz.'*

There was a sound from behind them. Magdalena was waking up. Gump knelt down beside her and Eva rushed over.

'Magdalena,' Gump said gently. 'Can you hear me?'

Her eyes flickered open and then shut. With a great effort she opened them again.

'Blanco?' she asked.

'He's fine,' said Gump, patting her hand reassuringly. 'You saved him.'

'She saved you?' Eva asked Blanco.

Blanco nodded. 'The Count tried to kill me when I followed you into the cave. Magdalena stopped him.'

Eva knelt by Magdalena and brushed her hair back from her forehead. Blanco squatted beside her.

'Thank you,' he said. 'I know if it wasn't for you, I'd be dead. I'm sorry I thought you had betrayed Eva.'

Eva looked surprised.

'I'll explain later,' said Blanco.

'Where is he?'

Magdalena was obviously talking about the Count. The effort of speaking weakened her and her eyes closed.

'He's gone after the stone.'

She opened her eyes and looked at Eva.

'You got it then?'

Eva nodded. 'But Rameel has stolen it and Luca and the Count have gone to find it. We have to go after them. I'm sorry.'

Magdalena understood from that they would be leaving her here.

'I'll stay with you,' said Gump, and she gave him a tremulous smile.

'Thank you,' she said.

★ ★ ★

Eva went back to Micha and this time the angel allowed her to put an arm round her. She felt colder than usual to the touch and her sadness was palpable. Eva could feel it seeping from her bones. Blanco stood next to them. He had a message for Micha from Azaz but he wasn't sure how to say it. He was intimidated by the sorrow on her face but he had promised.

'I have a message for you,' he said hesitantly. 'From Azaz.'

Micha lifted her golden face and Eva saw it was wet with tears. She had never seen an angel cry before. It was a terrible sight.

'He said you would understand what he had to do. He said to build a legend. He said you didn't have to wait but that, if you did, one day he would come out.'

Micha looked sad again. 'I'll wait,' she whispered.

'What does he mean?' asked Eva. 'What legend. Our legend?'

Micha shook her head. 'A new one,' she said. 'But you must go. You must find Luca.'

'Why is it so important that we find Luca?' asked Blanco. 'If the stone has no power?'

'It's not the philosopher's stone,' said Micha. 'But if Luca swallows the stone then he will turn back into an angel.'

Both Blanco and Eva gaped in astonishment.

'Luca's an angel?' spluttered Eva.

'He was.'

'Luca Ferron, Luca Ferron,' muttered Blanco behind her. 'Luca Ferr . . . Lucifer.'

'His punishment was different from ours,' said Micha. 'We were all punished for rebelling but his was more severe because he didn't just want to teach something or love somebody. He wanted to destroy everything. You can't let him swallow the stone. You can't risk him turning back into an angel. There's no telling what he'll do.'

'So he's a bad angel like Rameel.'

Micha shook her head. 'He's much much worse than Rameel. Rameel loved once even if it turned to bitterness. And he's starting to feel again. Because of you, Eva.'

'Me?'

'All these months of travelling with you has changed him, even though he tried to fight it.'

'What happens if Luca doesn't swallow the stone?' asked Blanco.

'He'll die. He's already dying. He'll die and be born again in some later age.'

'So we won't actually stop him.'

'All we can ever do is stop him in each lifetime that he is born into,' said Micha. 'That is our job. That was what Azaz and I agreed to do as our punishment. Azaz always said . . . ' Here her voice stumbled and she started to cry again.

'Micha,' said Blanco urgently. 'You must come with us. We need you. We can't deal with him alone.'

Once again, Micha shook her head. 'I can't leave Azaz,' she said, looking at them with tear-filled eyes. 'It's up to you. It's all up to you.'

At first, Eva and Blanco walked in silence, overwhelmed by what they'd just heard. Saifullah had told them that there was no way out of the valley except back through the village. That wouldn't be a problem for Rameel, of course, since he could fly, but Micha seemed convinced that Luca would find a way to call him back. And Luca wasn't an angel yet so he couldn't fly.

As they walked their hands brushed against each other and then they were holding hands. It made them both feel much better because they didn't know what they were going to find at the end of the valley.

Rameel tried to ignore the voice but it was too insistent. He clutched the heartstone to his chest and tried not to listen. He had his heart back and he was determined to hold on to it. He wasn't sure if he would bury it again. He didn't know what he wanted to do with it but he wasn't giving it to Lucifer, no matter how much he demanded it.

He tried to ignore Lucifer's voice but it was seeping into the outermost reaches of his mind, smothering everything else. It was calling him back.

Luca was standing right at the edge of the valley. It ended in a precipice. The Count was standing a little way behind him.

Eva had always been able to see Rameel but for the first time Blanco could also see the giant dark angel as well. He was hovering over the abyss where the precipice ended. He was still clutching the heartstone, his hands pressing it to his chest. He was looking down at it. He had never looked more beautiful.

Luca had his arms raised as though he was calling Rameel to him. Rameel, in turn, seemed to be floating towards him, as though pulled by an invisible string.

'What is he doing?' whispered Eva.

'It's as if he has him under a spell,' Blanco whispered back.

'What shall we do? If we go any closer the Count will see us.'

'What is he going to do?'

The answer to that came sooner than expected for as soon as Rameel came within reaching distance of Luca, the Count raced towards them. Luca turned as the Count approached and with a malicious smile on his face side-stepped as the Count reached him and gave him a push. With a scream of fear, the Count went over the edge.

'Magdalena,' said Gump. 'I'm sorry.'

He was holding her hand.

'What for?' she asked.

'For leaving you in Malta. For not coming back for you. I should never have believed you were dead without checking.'

Magdalena nodded. 'It wasn't your fault,' she said. 'I thought the same. Christobal was very persuasive. It was hard when Blanco told me that you were still alive and that you had married and had a family. But I'm glad you had a good life, a full life.'

Gump tightened his grip on her hand. 'I wish you had.'

'I did,' she said. 'In my own way. It doesn't matter

now. I know that you loved me once. That's what matters.'

'Not just once,' said Gump. 'Always. I always loved you. You were always in my heart.'

'As you were always in mine.'

She smiled at him and closed her eyes.

'Magdalena!' he said urgently.

There was no reply.

Blanco and Eva started running at the same time as the Count. Blanco dived as the Count went over the edge and just caught the trailing edge of his cloak. He felt it rip as the cloak came off but he could see—and feel—that the Count was hanging on to the other end. Blanco struggled with the weight. More of the cloak was vanishing over the edge—and it was pulling Blanco with it.

'Why do you bother?' asked Luca with real curiosity in his voice. 'You hate him. He hates you. He'd kill you in a moment. He's tried many times.'

'That was his decision,' said Blanco through gritted teeth. 'This is mine. I can't just let him fall.'

Luca raised his arms again and Rameel's great head lifted. His eyes were shut. His face was completely white; his long dark hair hung down his back. He was concentrating hard, trying to block out the call.

'Rameel!' shouted Eva urgently.

'Shut up!' said Luca angrily, his attention turning from Rameel to Eva.

'Rameel, wake up!' cried Eva.

Rameel's eyelids flickered.

Blanco made one final effort and the Count's hand appeared, scrabbling for purchase on the stony surface. Luca stamped down hard on the hand. With a scream the Count was forced to let go and his full weight hung for a moment on his cloak which Blanco was still clutching. The weight nearly pulled him over.

'Reach up,' he said desperately.

'I can't!'

'Try! Do you want to die? I thought you wanted the stone!'

With a desperate lunge, the Count's hand connected with Blanco's.

'Rameel! She forgives you. She told me she forgives you!' cried Eva.

She was still trying to get Rameel to wake up. She knew that by talking to him she was beginning to unblock the hold Luca had on his mind. She was terrified by what Micha had told her about Luca but she kept reminding herself that, at the moment, he was only a man. Not Lucifer. Just a man. And an old man at that. One who was getting older with every moment that passed.

Luca dropped his hands and turned to face Eva. She was interfering with his hold over Rameel. His bright blue eyes were colder than the heartstone had been when it turned to ice in her hands. She stepped back in fear, stumbled over a rock, and fell. Luca reached down and grabbed her, pulling her back to her feet.

'Blanco!' she screamed.

There was nothing Blanco could do. The Count was still hanging on. With a huge effort he finally managed to pull Count Maleficio over the edge of the precipice.

They lay breathlessly on the ground for a moment. In the struggle the Count had lost his cloak and without it he looked as insubstantial as a piece of string.

Rameel was still hovering above them all. Luca held Eva close.

'Good work, Luca,' said the Count, rising to his feet.

The Count still wasn't ready to give up on his partnership.

'We can still share the stone when you get it,' he said pleadingly.

'He just pushed you over the edge of the cliff,' called Blanco over his shoulder, as he ran to Eva's side. 'Do you really think he's going to share now?'

The Count shot him a furious look. Blanco might have just saved his life but that didn't mean that he had to like him.

Luca dragged Eva closer to the edge. She didn't dare look down.

'No closer, boy,' he snarled at Blanco.

'Let her go!' cried Blanco.

Luca ignored him.

'Leave her alone,' said Micha fiercely.

Luca glared up at her.

'Micha!' cried Eva in delight.

None of them had seen her approach.

'Love was always your weakness,' Luca said.

'Love is not a weakness,' she said. 'It's a strength. And if you had ever understood that then you would never have been trapped as you are. You would have got a lesser punishment.'

'This feeble body,' said Luca, pulling at his clothes. 'It does nothing except rot. I can't fly. I can't do anything.'

'You could love,' said Micha. 'You could try to live a full life.'

Luca spat out in disgust at the thought.

Eva struggled to break Luca's hold but even though he was weakening he was still stronger than she was.

Luca looked up. 'There's nothing you can do, Micha,' he said. 'You're too late.'

Turning, he faced the precipice and the angel hovering there.

'Rameel,' he called seductively. 'Rameel, come here.'

The dark angel slowly flew towards them. His large indigo wings swept up and down in beautiful graceful movements.

'Give me the stone,' said Luca.

Rameel's dark eyes snapped open. He held out his hand. The heartstone was balanced on it.

'No!' cried Blanco.

'Let the girl go,' said Rameel, surprising them all.

'No!' said Luca.

'You want the stone, don't you?'

Luca nodded reluctantly.

'Then let her go.'

'Rameel!' cried Micha. 'What are you doing?'

Rameel looked at Micha and for a moment she was sure he winked at her. But he said nothing and turned his attention back to Luca.

Luca pushed Eva in Blanco's direction. Blanco quickly grabbed her and pulled him to her.

'You want this?' asked Rameel, holding it out to Luca and the Count. 'Try and take it.'

The Count and Luca both dashed forward, pushing each other out of the way like squabbling children. Blanco wondered if he should try to stop them but a movement from Micha stopped him.

'Look.'

Blanco squeezed Eva's shoulder to get her attention. Rameel was holding out the stone, which was changing as Rameel held it there. It was shrinking before their eyes.

'It's melting!'

The heart, so long frozen, now exposed to the light, was soaking up the warmth of the sun and going the way of all frozen things. It was transforming into something else.

The Count was the first to reach Rameel. He stretched out a hand and tried to take the stone but he dropped it almost immediately. Rameel caught it and laughed. He held it out again. The stone was melting quickly, losing its colour and its shape. Luca howled in frustration as every time he tried to pick it up it slipped through his fingers. His face was becoming more lined and his hands more shaky. Even when all that was left was a pool of water he kept grabbing at Rameel's hand.

Eventually Rameel turned his hand over and a pool of water spilled from it onto the ground. As it fell the sunlight caught it and it was like myriad rainbows falling to earth. He smiled sadly as he watched it go.

Luca crawled to the spot where the water had fallen but the earth had already soaked it up. He clutched his chest and collapsed on the ground, his skin growing whiter by the moment. 'No,' he said. 'I won't go through this again.'

'It looks as if you have no choice,' said Micha.

As they watched, Luca's eyes closed and he lay still.

* * *

They found Gump sitting by Magdalena's body. Eva was distraught when she found out that Magdalena had died while they weren't there. Blanco led her away, leaving Gump and the Count to deal with Magdalena together. The Count was a broken man. He had lost his one true love and the dream of power and riches which he had been chasing for twenty years. Even Gump felt sorry for him.

'Eva.'

Eva looked up. She and Blanco had been sitting against a rock; she had been crying and he was comforting her. Her tears had stopped and she was sitting with her head resting on Blanco's shoulder.

Micha sank down to the ground in front of them, her long white robes flowing out around her.

'Eva,' she said. 'You know I can't come with you any more.'

Eva looked shocked. She hadn't thought of that. In the last few hours she had gained her greatest wish—Blanco—but had also lost two of the people who meant the most to her—Azaz and Magdalena. Now Micha was telling her that she was going to lose her too.

'Why?'

Micha held out a hand to Eva and Eva took it. 'Azaz is still in there,' she said. 'Do you remember what I told you about angels being underground?'

'You said that you can't breathe,' she said.

'Azaz will have to stay underground until he gets his energy back,' she said. 'It may take a thousand years. I have to wait for him.'

Eva gulped and nodded. 'What will I do without you?' she asked. The angels had been with her for years. Without them she would be alone.

'*You don't need me any more,*' said Micha. '*You've got someone else to look after you.*'

Blanco took Eva's other hand.

'I'll always look after you,' he said fiercely. 'Always.'

Epilogue

Venice—a year later

Blanco stood at the front of the gondola and watched the church draw near.

'Stop fretting,' said a voice from behind him. 'We've got plenty of time.'

Blanco turned round to face his great-uncle. 'I've seen Eva try to get married twice before,' he said. 'Something's always gone wrong.'

Gump laughed. 'That something has usually been you,' he said.

Count Maleficio had not returned with them from Badakhshan. He had decided to stay in the mountains to build a memorial to Magdalena. He had promised that he wouldn't teach the miners how to use the fire-powder. Blanco didn't believe him but there was little he could do about it. About two months after they had returned to Venice, Gump received a message. It had been passed from merchant to traveller, pilgrim to priest, and across mountains, deserts, and seas by the time it reached his hands. The note was from Saifullah and explained how the Count had broken his promise almost immediately. He and Faisal had tried to build a beast but in testing it had blown themselves up.

But he had good news too. The miners were already telling a story about an angel trapped within the mountain and another one waiting outside. No one had actually seen Micha but many of the miners had felt her presence. They were both seen as lucky spirits. Since then the mountain had been producing better stones than ever.

'A new legend,' said Gump, looking up from the letter.

'What do you mean?' asked Blanco.

'That's how legends grow,' said Gump. 'From a simple story.'

'So they'll always be remembered,' said Eva, who was there too. 'I like that.'

They had never heard from Rameel again.

With the letter was also a small gift for Eva and Blanco. Gump had kept that a secret. He was saving that for a special day. A day like today.

Standing on the church steps Blanco could see many familiar faces. His own family stood at the front. His father still couldn't see and his hand was resting on his wife's shoulder. They were both smiling happily. Angelica stood beside them—dressed as a girl, Blanco was thankful to see. Their father had accepted that she had kept the business going and was still allowing her to run it, although he had insisted that she stopped dressing as a boy.

Eva stood alone in the middle of the steps. She had tried to forbid her family to come to the wedding but

Blanco had insisted that she should try to forgive them. Hadn't they seen enough, he reasoned, of what bitterness could do to people? Hadn't Luca and the Count shown them that? Reluctantly, Eva had agreed, but she refused to allow them to stand next to her on the steps.

The gondola reached the steps and Blanco leapt out. He cast a quick look round to make sure that there were no unwelcome guests. He still couldn't believe that Count Maleficio and Luca Ferron were no longer chasing them. He looked at Eva standing on the steps and thought of all that they had gone through together. As he ran up the steps to stand beside her a little gust of wind blew something in front of him. Picking them up, Blanco found two feathers—one red and one gold. Smiling, he handed them to Eva.

'Azaz! Micha!'

Eva looked up at the sky but could see nothing.

Her father raised his eyes to heaven, praying that the many guests wouldn't notice his daughter's strange behaviour—again. Blanco laughed at the look on his face. He didn't care if everyone thought his wife-to-be was crazy. He knew she wasn't. He knew she was the bravest, most lovable, and annoying person he had ever met.

Eva knew the angels were there, somewhere, always watching over her. She turned and smiled at Blanco. He took her hand and they turned to face the priest.

When it came time for the rings to be exchanged, Blanco smiled with delight as he took the ring which Gump handed him. As Blanco placed the ring on Eva's finger the gold reflected the sunshine. Caught in its centre was a tiny bit of the night sky with one shining star within its depths. It was their very own heartstone.

HAZEL MARSHALL was born in Scotland and has lived there for most of her life, with occasional breaks to go travelling. When not writing, Hazel works for the BBC. She currently lives in London, although writing the *Troublesome Angels* trilogy has given her very itchy feet.

Troublesome Angels Race to the Rescue is Hazel's third novel, and it follows the exciting *Troublesome Angels and Flying Machines* and *Troublesome Angels and the Red Island Pirates*.